Praise for *Think of England*

"Everything in this spare, eccentrically paced book is a pleasure to read.... It's almost impossible to write about the kind of subtle, inward sorrows and tensions that animate this story, and the author manages the challenge handsomely."

—*The New Yorker*

"Alice Elliott Dark has such a reputation as a master storyteller, it comes as something of a surprise to realize that this is her first novel. Her story weaves together the themes of death, guilt, and the individuality that somehow binds family members together while simultaneously pulling them apart. Dark's charm as a writer comes from her easy confidence. Here she never seems rushed, she never tries too hard to get a reaction."

—Ken Foster, *San Francisco Chronicle*

"What a winsome, winning first novel this is—so filled with memorable characters . . . the reader rejoices."

—Susan Larson, *The Times-Picayune*

"[Dark] has a gift for the perfectly chosen detail."

—Jamie Spencer, *St. Louis Post-Dispatch*

"Dark delicately constructs the enduring web of filial dynamics in her debut novel, quietly tackling the grievances that are passed down through the generations."

—Allyssa Lee, *Entertainment Weekly*

"A book whose grace notes . . . are true and many."

—Beth Kephart, *Baltimore Sun*

THINK OF ENGLAND

A NOVEL

ALICE ELLIOTT DARK

Simon & Schuster
New York London Toronto
Sydney Singapore

Dar

For Asher

SIMON & SCHUSTER
Rockefeller Center
1230 Avenue of the Americas
New York, NY 10020

First Simon & Schuster trade paperback edition 2003

SIMON & SCHUSTER and colophon are registered trademarks
of Simon & Schuster, Inc.

For information regarding special discounts for bulk purchases,
please contact Simon & Schuster Special Sales at
1-800-456-6798 or business@simonandschuster.com

Designed by Jeanette Olender
Manufactured in the United States of America

1   3   5   7   9   10   8   6   4   2

The Library of Congress has cataloged the hardcover edition as follows:
Dark, Alice Elliott.
Think of England : a novel / Alice Elliott Dark.
p.   cm.
I. Title.
PS3554.A714 T48 2002
813'.54—dc21   2002017554
ISBN 0-684-86522-x
0-7432-3497-9 (Pbk)

8/03
BOT

THANKS

What a relief it is to have the support of good friends. Among mine are my sublime editor, the lovely Denise Roy; my valued agent, Henry Dunow, a mensch among men; and my dear and brilliant husband, Larry Dark. Without them, this book would still be just a lump in my throat.

Set me as a seal upon your heart . . .

for love is as strong as death,

passion as fierce as the grave.

Song of Solomon

Just close your eyes and think of England.

*Wedding-night advice for
Victorian brides*

1964

1964

ON THAT NIGHT, a Sunday in February, Jane read under the covers with a flashlight, skimming a novel for a page she wanted to read again. Every so often, she closed the book and looked at the cover, where her own name appeared in the title. It was exciting to see it that way, in carved letters. It made the book hers. She had a pen and her notebook with her, too, just in case; she liked to write things down. She was the kind of girl who felt New Year's should be in the fall, at the beginning of school, the kind of girl who begged for chores and saved quarters in a jar to buy a pony. Beneath her nightgown she wore a pair of fresh underpants—she'd spent the night with a girl who put them on before bed and she'd copied the idea. As usual she'd braided her hair to make it look smoother for school. Her brother Sean slept in the other bed, flat on his back with his hands dangling. Their little sister and brother—twins—were in their room down the hall. At nine Jane had begun to want a room of her own. She was writing a book.

For a while there was noise and music downstairs, and then the adults came up. Her father's footsteps, and Uncle

Francis's, were discernible, but it was only because she knew what to listen for that Jane was able to track Via, her mother, who had a habit of going barefoot in the house. Via's movements were dreamy and for the most part silent, but her bracelets gave away her whereabouts. She always wore three thick gold bracelets, even in the ocean and the shower. Slave bracelets, she called them.

The footsteps stopped outside her door. "Good night, sleep tight—or not," said Uncle Francis to Emlin and Via. He was spending the night in the guest room just on the other side of Jane's wall.

Via giggled. "You're bad!"

"I should hope so. I try, at least."

"Sshh! I'm going to check on them," Emlin said.

Jane shut off her flashlight. The door opened quietly, and in floated her father's head, a dark balloon.

"Misses?" he whispered.

She hesitated for a second. But he would never suspect her of deceiving him, so she couldn't do it. "Yes?"

"I thought you'd be up." He groped his way to the edge of her bed and sat down. She smelled his cigarettes and Scotch and, faintly, Royal Lyme. "Were we too noisy?"

"No. I was reading."

"Sean asleep?"

"Uh-huh."

"Is this your leg?"

Jane pushed the switch on the flashlight and it shone up through the blankets and his hand. He laughed. "I guess not. I thought it felt funny."

Jane switched the light off again. "You're not going to the hospital?"

"Nope. No emergencies tonight, at least not so far. Are you ready to go to sleep?"

"Soon." She knew he'd accept that. He wasn't as insistent on a good night's sleep as Via because he barely slept himself. He was a heart surgeon. Dr. MacLeod, pronounced "Ma-Cloud," which had to be explained to nearly everyone. Via's real name was Olivia.

"Okay. Soon," he repeated. He bent to kiss her. She pressed her cheek against his and moved her face so she could feel his scratchy whiskers. He began to pull away, but she reached out and circled his neck with her arms and he stayed, patting her back. Somehow it was like summer. His breathing like waves. She wanted him to stay all night. It was a sacrifice to let go, and she felt holy when she made herself do it.

"My girl." He patted her leg, and then the flashlight. She gave a small laugh to let him know she got the joke, and then she thought, quickly, of something to keep him there.

"I wrote a poem today," she said.

"You did?"

"About when I was born."

There was a pause. "Are you and your friends talking about that?"

"No. I remembered it."

"What did you remember?"

She knew what she'd written in the poem, but that wasn't the same as telling it. It was hard to explain. "Do you want to read it?" she asked.

"Tomorrow," he said. "As soon as I come home." He stood up and opened the door.

"Who was your favorite Beatle?" she whispered. "Mine was George."

"Oh, me too. "Definitely George. Don't stay up too late."

"Leave the door open?"

"All right."

She watched him walk down the hall. Beyond him she could see Via sitting on the bed, bending her head forward as she unfastened her necklace. Emlin waved as he shut their door. It was one of those nights when Jane heard not just the click of the catch, but also the scratching of metal as the lock slid into place. All she could see then was a thin line of light in the crack beneath their door. Light for a few moments, and then darkness. She turned her flashlight back on.

. . .

It was a frigid month in eastern Pennsylvania, but the field-stone house held the heat well and ponderous quilts coated the children's beds. Yet Jane felt the cold. When she moved even slightly, she touched gelid spots of sheeting, and when she emerged for air, her nose grew numb and rubbery. She reached for her notebook. *The MacMillans will get caught in a twister*, she wrote. At her school they used connected printing, but she was teaching herself cursive. She'd written her poem in cursive.

Sean murmured, and Jane listened to see whether or not he was only talking in his sleep. He was eleven months younger than Jane, her Irish twin—except that they weren't

Irish. They were of English and Scots descent, with drops of German and French, and, Jane liked to think, American Indian. Emlin's grandfather had been a doctor among the Sioux in South Dakota, on what became the Rosebud Reservation. She thought something, some deep tie, must have drawn him there. The tie of family.

She and Sean didn't look much alike; Sean was brown-eyed and ruddy, like Via, while Jane was said to look like Emlin's mother. Jane stared and stared in the mirror, trying to see that tiny old woman reflected back at her, but there were only her own green eyes, her crooked teeth—she'd just gotten braces—and her thin, tangly pale hair, which Via had her wear pushed back with a plastic hairband that gave her headaches. In the summer she had freckles, which surprised her every year. She was tall, with long legs and, as Via could foresee, her father's artless elegance. In recent months she'd begun to dress like a boy; there was more freedom to being a boy.

When Sean kept babbling, Jane sighed and went to sit by him. She was a watchful child, whereas Sean was, according to Via, mischievous. He got into trouble, but he also made Via laugh.

She pulled his blanket up. "Sshh, shhh," into his ear, until he settled down.

She went back to her own bed and was awakened sometime later by a shout. Around the edges of the shades the sky was obsidian; still night.

Sean murmured again. Via said he slept like a wrestler wrestled.

"Go back to sleep," Jane whispered. "Everything's fine."

She closed her bedroom door behind her and stood in the hall, her feet curling away from the chilly floor. She felt a presence nearby; Uncle Francis was standing in the doorway of the guest room, listening. Presently there was another shout, bleak and full of anguish, coming from her parents' bedroom.

"Go back to bed," Francis whispered, but when Jane didn't move, he reached for her hand.

. . .

Francis Gordon had come to the MacLeod's house that day for two reasons: one, because he'd ended an affair, and needed a break from his apartment and the scents and mementos it still contained. The other reason was that he wanted to watch the Beatles' performance on *The Ed Sullivan Show* in the company of his sister, Via, with whom he could share a self-regarding excitement that he didn't trust anyone else to stimulate. He'd seen the Beatles in Hamburg on one of his louche trips abroad. He'd seen them in a scruffy, dank club—at the time, they were scruffy, dank boys—and came back telling everyone they'd be famous. No one listened; he'd had to be a bore and remind his cynical friends of his prescience when he turned out to be right. Via, on the other hand, had called him the instant she read about them in the paper. "Isn't that the group you told me about?" She was a match for his own, if disguised, romanticism, except that he configured himself as dashing while she dreamed of the adoration of a dashing man.

As he'd expected, Via was thrilled to have him, especially as Emlin had gone off to the hospital. When she arrived at the station just before noon, the car brimming with children in coats and boots and mittens and scarves, she greeted him with such a look of ironic despair that he precipitously tipped all the cards he'd planned to hold to his chest and lay down one by one—he imagined Via pleading for details—over the course of the afternoon. The persona he'd created of a searing aesthete, biceps enlarged by his burden of weltschmerz, evaporated around her. She'd known him when he was just a goofball.

"Dumped again," he said merrily.

Via handed him a cig and they lit up together. "Me, too," she said. "For a seventeen-year-old from Australia, no less."

It took an instant for him to figure out that she was referring to one of Emlin's patients. He spread his arm like a languid cat along the top of the seat and cuffed her shoulder.

"You win," he said, ready to forget New York, to have Via play with him.

She turned to him. "Do I? What prize is that? The prize for having made the biggest mistake?"

He wanted to keep laughing, but she was serious. He realized he'd come on a bad day; from the depth of her tone—low, exasperated, defeated—he guessed all the days had become bad ones.

She jerked the wheel hard toward the exit, and he turned to say hello to the children.

"So how about it?" He was big, loud, merry.

"Hi," they said shyly, and stared out at the parking lot.

. . .

Jane was expected at her friend Susan's in half an hour; Via decided to kill the wait by driving around. Francis, who hadn't been to Wynnemoor in quite a while, groaned at the harsh sensations brought on by the sights.

"I'm in *hell*," he hissed as they passed the blunt orange brick buildings of his old school.

Via blew a plume of smoke at the windshield. "No, you're just visiting. I'm the permanent resident."

"You know what your problem is," Francis said. "You're too avid."

Jane opened her notebook. The last episode had the MacMillans sitting on their terrace drinking lemonade after chasing a burglar away. Instinctively, she understood *avid*.

"You have to play harder to get," Francis said matter-of-factly.

Via depressed the turn signal. Her smallest gestures had flair; she could wear hats with net veils over her eyes and not look pretentious. "How am I supposed to do that, when I already married him?"

Sean began to read aloud. "'I think I better stay home from work for a while, in case the burglar comes back,' said Mr. MacMillan."

Jane snapped the notebook shut. "Stop peeking!" She opened it again, but higher this time, and shifted to face him so he could only see the outside cover.

Francis rolled his eyes. "God, are you a ninny. You have no idea how much power you have, do you? Look, you have to decide what you want, and then plan how to get it."

"And this method works for you?" Via sat up straighter and peered ahead, as if she'd spotted something in front of the car. It was difficult to tell if she was teasing or being cruel.

Francis chose not to take offense. "Even an idiot can tell you when you have a hole in the back of your sweater."

"I suppose." Via turned the wheel sharply and the children listed like dominoes toward the left door.

"Oh God." Francis clapped his hands over his eyes. "You're torturing me on purpose, aren't you?

Via was pleased with herself. "See? I'm capable of carrying out a plan."

They approached the dour gray edifice of the Church of St. Paul. The children righted themselves. Jane decided against reading anymore and tucked her notebook inside her jacket.

"No!" Francis made a cross with his index fingers, as if warding off a vampire, and held it up toward the steeple. Then he dropped his hands. "That's not going to work, is it?"

Via giggled. She twisted toward the back seat while keeping her eyes on the road. "Children, did you know Uncle Francis was an altar boy?"

"Hold your breath or you'll have bad luck!" Sean ordered as they glided past the pretty yard of snow-capped graves.

. . .

After playing outside for a while and eating a lunch of grilled cheese sandwiches, Jane and Susan did their homework. An author would be in their class the next day and they had to write something to show her. Jane's stomach purled when she thought about it. She could see herself at the front of the room, reading aloud, reading well, receiving praise from a stranger that might change how she was seen; but she could also imagine being passed over. It mystified her that she was unable to make herself known. Her head clamored all the time with loud ideas. How was it that no one noticed?

When she and Susan became friends on the first day of kindergarten, they were the same. Within a few weeks there was a difference. The teachers and children issued an unspoken invitation to be at the center of all things that happened in the room. Susan received it. Jane didn't. Why?

Susan's hair, for one thing. At recess girls asked her if they could braid it, but it was so slippery that no braid would hold. The buttery strands unraveled until they were all across Susan's back again, a sunny curtain.

And the way she talked. Teachers smiled. Over and over, they said she had a good imagination.

The teachers said little about Jane. The green eyes her grandfather called the windows of her soul were nothing. She'd started off with the wrong clothes.

"Why do you want to be a sheep?" Via asked.

"I don't." Jane dipped her chin and hugged her own ribs. It was hard to explain. Via let her choose her dresses and she'd chosen wrong. "I need a Fair Isle sweater. I'm going to wear my kilt."

"I thought you said it was too itchy."

It was, but Jane wanted to be able to complain about it, along with everyone else.

She had friends now; she'd figured out how to do it. But she still wasn't seen, not really. She was a burning shadow.

In Susan's room she settled on the window seat, her back pressed against the molding, her notebook propped on her knees. Susan lay on the floor. Susan's indifference to the window seat never failed to astonish Jane. She thought if she had one, she'd sit there all the time.

During the past couple of months, the backyard had been made peculiar by snow. The change didn't faze her; she shied away only from slush, and the black-flecked boulders banked along the main streets. She watched the birds dive toward the feeder and studied the surely drawn lines of animal tracks to see if there was anything out there other than pets. It began to snow again. She made a game of counting the flakes as they appeared at the window until there were too many falling at once. The new snow began to stick to the old crust, and the birds took a last seed before seeking shelter. A line of fresh snow trimmed the beam at the top of the swing set. She stared at the scene, playing with her vision and making it blurry until her focus began to shift.

Suddenly she was tumbling helplessly in a wave, then inching through a dark passage, breathless. Through eyes still mucked up and blurry, she saw her mother and she breathed. Everything was bright, and people, a doctor and nurses, handled her like a football and cleaned blood and gunk off her as if she were a muddy shoe. She recognized the images; she'd always remembered being born. When she was six, she'd described it to Via, who hadn't believed her. Since then she'd kept the memory to herself, but now it begged for form, pressed at her chest and arm, until she picked up her notebook and wrote.

She wrote from a voice that spoke in complete lines; she wrote fast, as if she were a secretary taking dictation. When she reread the page, she couldn't believe it had come from her. It was like nothing she'd ever written before. It was a real poem.

She saw what Monday would be like; the teacher would call her to the front of the room and the author would praise her in front of everyone. She saw herself describing how it felt to write it. So significant.

Susan groaned and rolled onto her side. "That's finished," she said. "Wanna play checkers?"

Jane was far away, so far that at first she didn't understand what Susan said. She was caught up in a new language, the grammar of creation.

"Jane? Are you okay?"

That got through; Jane flew back to Earth, Wynnemoor, the Roberts's house, the window seat. Part of her wanted to read the poem to Susan right away, but it didn't really go with a game of checkers. Solemnly she closed her notebook. Susan would have to be surprised along with everyone else.

AT FOUR-THIRTY Emlin arrived to pick Jane up. She heard the bell ring, and then Emlin talking downstairs with Susan's mother in his low, soft, slightly Southern voice. Jane and Susan were in the upstairs hall, playing jacks. Jane didn't run down right away, however, but behaved instead the way a girl would for whom it was normal to have an available father. She kept playing, and waited.

"Jane? Your father's here." Mrs. Roberts's footsteps sounded on the lower stairs as she sought a better vantage point for her announcement. "Jane?"

She stopped to listen for a response, and for a moment the house was utterly quiet. Jane felt Susan look at her, but she refused to look back; she didn't want to break the spell. It was only a second or two, however, before she realized she'd unwittingly taken Uncle Francis's romantic advice. She was acting hard-to-get. "Coming!" she called out, and stood up. She didn't want to play one of Francis's tricks on her father.

She hurried down the steps. They were both watching her; they'd run out of conversation. Emlin looked handsome.

23

"Daddy," she said, taking his hand. "How was your patient?"

"She's okay. A little weak. Jane's my chief nurse," he said to Mrs. Roberts.

"She came all the way from Australia just to be operated on by him." Jane leaned against his side proprietarily.

Susan joined them.

"Hi, Dr. MacLeod." She elbowed Jane. "You forgot your notebook."

"I did?" She turned to run back upstairs.

"Wait." Susan pulled it from behind her back, and Jane took it and held it against her chest. "We did our homework," Susan told the adults.

Emlin and Mrs. Roberts smiled at each other in a broad, buoyant manner. How nice to have homework. How fun to spend a snowy afternoon with a friend.

. . .

"Boy, am I tired," Emlin said. "I could sleep for a week."

She twisted to see his face. He laid a hand on her shoulder.

"Uncle Francis is here," she told him.

Emlin raised his eyebrows. "There goes sleep."

She sat on the front seat close to him, and as the heat began to blow, she stretched her hands toward the vents. The gray of the afternoon was deepening to charcoal, and in all the pretty, large houses, the windows shone with warm affirming light. From time to time she was able to see people inside, women walking briskly. Her friends lived in many of the places they passed, and she craned to spot them up in their bedrooms, and noticed peripherally the silhouettes of the huge, dark pines and spruces, stalwart in the cold. They passed her grandparents' road, and the house with the whippets, and the dead-end street with the brick gate at its entrance that was lined with new low ranch houses and trees that had been plonked in the ground fully grown. Instant landscapes. They knew no one who lived up there.

Their neighborhood had no name. It was in the southern part of Wynnemoor, which was itself a charm on the bracelet of towns surrounding Philadelphia. Roomy houses loomed among the trees both up and below the rolling hills, belying such concepts as lots and property lines—who knew where one place ended and the next began? The rich Pennsylvania soil, sprinkled with glittering shards of mica, was good for gardening and for thick, cool lawns strewn with clover and tiny blue Quaker-ladies. Flowers, even roses, grew easily, with little care, so everyone grew them. Emlin gave Via a lilac bush for their fifth anniversary. Now, six years later, it bloomed fragrant wands in the early spring that bent, heavy with dew in the early mornings, to the children's noses.

In the winter landscape, fern pods and dried astilbe leaned their brittle spines toward the pale sun, boxwood and rose sat swathed in burlap, shiny holly bushes rattled in the wind flashing their hard red berries, snow-burdened limbs of various fir species drooped, and here and there along any road, seeping through the clear cold air, there was the beckoning scent of a hearth fire.

Emlin craned the wheel to turn into Willow Lane, then again into their driveway. As he moved his arms, he gave off the smell of hospital. The wreath was still on the door from Christmas. The red door shone beneath the porch light. Jane had had her doubts when Via first announced she was going to paint it red, but it turned out to be beautiful. If anything, it seemed even a better idea in the winter, when it was the one bright red dot in the scene—like a Corot, Uncle Francis said. Lights glowed from every window in shapes made various by the pulling of curtains and the lowering of shades. Anyone driving by would think the people living there were lucky.

Emlin shifted to park in front of the garage door. "Ready, Misses? Or should we go out to dinner somewhere? That would be fun, wouldn't it?"

Jane considered this. It was tempting to have dinner alone with her father, and to postpone going inside. But the others were waiting for them, and for Jane the pull of expectation was an unavailing gravity.

"What about the Beatles?"

He drummed his index fingers on the steering wheel. "Good point. We wouldn't want to miss that."

Jane ignored the tease; she was thinking. The MacMillans should call the police. The burglar should get caught.

. . .

"Back from the wars!" Uncle Francis called out from the living room. In the hall Jane and Emlin stomped their snowy boots on the mat as they stowed away the hallowed feeling of their hushed drive home. Emlin hung up their coats and Angus came bounding from the kitchen. He jumped up happily, his black nails making marks on Jane's corduroys. He was a West Highland white terrier, five years old.

"Yes," Jane said to him, ruffling his neck, "yes. I missed you, too."

"Come join us!" Francis called.

They obeyed him, Angus trotting alongside. The living room glowed with candles and low light. Via was seated at one end of the sofa, near the rustling fire, while Francis perched on the arm at the other end. Even seen from a distance, one would guess they were brother and sister. It was most evident in their postures, the easy way they held themselves, their infectious laughs, as if they expected to be welcomed wherever they went. (*I'm attractive, not pretty*, Via said, *which is better in the long run*.) They looked English, with their brown hair and fair, pink-cheeked skin. Francis was four years older, but seemed still unrooted and therefore somehow young, the way people often do who don't want children. He was openly homosexual, although he spared his parents the details and did what he could not to embarrass them, a policy that included not coming to Wynnemoor much anymore. He scoffed when Via said she'd disappointed her parents; she couldn't begin to compete with the blot he'd made on the escutcheon. Francis knew that when his father looked at him, he was thinking *remittance man*. It was the only word Hamish Gordon knew for what Francis was. Francis liked to joke that he'd gladly accept the label if an actual remittance went along with it. As it was, he was on his own. Via was twenty-nine.

She beckoned to Jane. She was dressed up in a skirt and

stockings and a cashmere sweater. And makeup, even on her eyelids. Her Joy perfume. She seemed happy. She touched her fingers to Jane's hips and guided her around to a place on the sofa beside her. Automatically, Jane reached to spin Via's heavy gold bracelets.

"What are the other children doing?" Emlin asked. He'd stopped short of joining the tableau.

Via stiffened. "Hello to you, too. I don't know. Building bombs?" She jiggled her crossed leg.

Emlin frowned. "I'm going to go change. I'll check on them."

When he'd left, Via sighed. "He's checking up on me, not them. He doesn't trust me with *his* children."

"Never mind," Francis said lightly. He leaned closer. "Or should I say, *Think of England*?" He straightened up, grinning.

"Please don't. Even coming from you it makes me cringe."

Think of England was what Nonny, Jane's grandmother —their mother—said in the event of any hitch in the proceedings, be it a full-blown crisis or misplaced keys. Jane wondered what was wrong with the saying—it made her think of warm fields brimming with wildflowers and small, unblinking animals—but knew better than to talk about Nonny with her mother.

"I don't think that particular homily is original to her," Francis said. "But I'll rephrase. Ignore him. We're going to have fun tonight."

"Fun? What's that?"

Jane let the bracelets settle and tucked her hands under her legs.

Uncle Francis pretended Via's question was another joke, a small one that didn't require laughter and could be swiftly let go. He plunked off the arm of the sofa and landed in the seat, intending to make Jane smile. She did, politely. He raised his leg and pulled his thick calf toward him with his hands, putting one ankle on the other knee. Jane looked at the hairless patch of white skin between his sock and his pants. "Now you, talk to me. Tell all. What's it like to be nine these days?"

She shrugged.

"That thrilling, eh? Well, it gets better. Or at least more interesting. Here, have one." He held toward her an open silver cigarette case.

"No, thank you."

"Come on," Francis waved the case. "It's time you get certain skills under your belt. You don't want to have to learn everything when you're already a grown up, do you?"

"Believe me, you don't," Via said, raising her drink in a toast. "Here's to skills!"

Jane gazed up at her. *Too much alcohol*, she thought. *Again.*

Francis put the case back inside his jacket. "Let me know if you change your mind," he said to Jane. "I'm your god-father as well as your uncle, remember, which saddles me with certain responsibilities. It's my duty to see that you're equipped for life in this rather heartbreaking world." He picked his glass up off the end table and rattled the ice. "It would be nice if you were smarter about things than we've been."

"I think you're smart," Jane said.

Via grimaced. "Hah! Shows how much you know." She sipped at her brown drink without looking at either of them.

"Thank you, Jane," Francis said, "for that vote of confidence." He looked at her, probing. "I'm being flip. Do you know what that is?"

He always spoke to her differently than other adults did. She shrugged.

"It's not a good way to be," he said. "It's a lame substitute for honesty. But it's the best I can do right now. Do you understand?"

She nodded so he'd let her look away.

"Understand what?"

Emlin stopped in the doorway and leaned against the jamb, putting all his weight on one leg. He had thick, painful varicose veins that the children stroked as if they were living creatures. He'd changed into slacks and a turtleneck sweater and leather slippers with no backs.

"Nothing. Idle chatter."

"So?" Via said. "How are they?"

"They're fine. Playing with the Lincoln Logs."

"I'm with them all the time. I can sense when something's wrong."

Jane thought, that's mostly true, but not always.

"If you saw what I see . . ." Emlin shook his head, as if his knowledge was unbearable.

Via frowned. "Please. Spare me tales of the emergency room."

"I second that." Francis raised his glass. "Come join us, Em. I was just having the most delightful conversation with your lovely daughter."

He proffered his cigarette case to Emlin, who came over, chose one, and held it between his lips. Uncle Francis took one, too, then spun his lighter and Emlin bent toward the flame. He is elegant, Jane thought, remembering what Nonny had said of Fred Astaire. For a moment the men were silhouetted, facing each other, Emlin with his classical profile and Francis, the more rugged of the two, looking as though he should be in work clothes rather than muscling against the seams of his gabardine suit. He lived in New York and worked at the Metropolitan Museum of Art.

"So what did you and the famous Susan do this afternoon?" Francis asked.

"We had to write something for school."

"May I read it?"

"Well—"

"It's useless, Francis," Via said abruptly. "She never shows anything. Although you're going to have to get over that, Jane. It's stupid to be shy."

"Besides, I know a lot of people in publishing." Francis spoke in a singsong that hinted at a quid pro quo. "And a lot of real writers."

"Jane's a real writer," Emlin said. "Aren't you, Misses?"

"I don't know." She couldn't bear to look at Via. She squeezed her thighs together and pressed her arms against her ribs. She fought back by competing; if her mother made her feel small, she'd make herself even smaller.

Francis raised his eyebrows. "Ah, youthful ambitions and dreams of glory. I remember that. I think. Or maybe I'm thinking of the famous tales of my father, the walking, talking Horatio Alger personification?" He and Via exchanged rueful grimaces. "Who knows where the parent ends and the child begins?" He pulled a stream of smoke up his nose.

"Don't even say that." Via shuddered.

"All right. I won't." He stubbed his cigarette into the heavy crystal ashtray Emlin and Via had received as a wedding present. It had the date engraved in the glass. Jane had once cut her finger trying to read it like braille. "And what are you going to write about, in the future, if you're a writer?" He tapped his handsome jaw with his fingers, tap, tap, tap. "How about this? A young man of brilliance and great good looks has his heart broken by a cad from the big city."

"Francis!" Via scolded, although she was smiling.

"Francis," Emlin echoed, far more grave.

The phone rang in the den. Emlin jumped up.

"No!" Via shouted. "Don't get it!" She reached to grab him, but he was too far away. "Don't!"

Emlin stood. "I have to, Olivia. You know that."

"But you just came *back* from the hospital! You can't go in again."

They stared at each other across a chasm of diverging logic, all the misunderstandings between them crammed between rings of the phone. They stared and wondered how she could possibly mistake life and death for a stubborn whim, how he could care more about strangers than his own family. They knew they had a guest, and that one of their children was watching them anxiously, but they were locked in a brute tug-of-war, beyond the reach of knowledge or other people. They were desperate.

At the next ring, Emlin rushed out, his slippers snapping against the soles of his feet.

Via flopped against the cushions and pulled a throw pillow into her lap, absentmindedly tracing the geometric bargello pattern. "All I can say is, goddamn Mr. Alexander Graham Bell. He's ruining my life!"

Francis kept his concern from his tone. "This from the girl who used to pay me to stay away from the phone in case one of her swains might call."

"I know," Via said. "But I'm too young to be alone, aren't I?"

"No one's marriage is great when there are small children in the house. Give it time."

"What do you think I've been doing? But how can I compete against people whose hearts are literally broken? He can sew them up and walk away. I'm a harder case. Chronic. He thinks I should—"

As she spoke, Jane got up and walked around the back of the sofa where Emlin had sat, past the piano, out of the room. She bent to pick up her notebook from where she'd left it against a wall in the hall. She could hear Sean upstairs telling the twins to hand him his Matchbox cars. In the den, Emlin was still on the telephone.

"I'll ask Via and let you know when would be a good time," he was saying.

With a sense of jubilance, she ran back into the living room. Angus jumped with excitement.

"It's not the hospital! It's not the hospital!"

Via shrugged, her mouth pinched. She wasn't as pleased as Jane had expected. "Then it's probably his mother," she said to Francis, making a face. "I'm not sure which is worse."

"The mother is always worse—present company excepted, of course."

"No, no. I don't think I'm going to get off the hook. Am I, Jane?" She raised her fingers in a V, for a fresh cig.

"I don't know. I've got homework." Jane twisted a strand of hair into a tight cord.

"Homework. I wish that were the extent of *my* problems." Via stretched out, plonking her feet on Francis's lap. The dark band at the top of her stocking showed. Jane was embarrassed for her.

"May I please be excused?" she asked.

"Go ahead," said Francis. "Remember, I want to see that book someday!"

. . .

At dinner Francis teased the twins, teaching them silly versions of table manners. They were Grand's jokes; Francis had stolen them. But Via giggled as if she'd never seen the routine before.

"And here's how you wipe your mouth," Francis said, and he sawed his napkin across the lower half of his face.

Via served spaghetti, her "Sunday night off" meal, as she called it, but the children barely touched it, Francis was too hilarious. The twins were splotched with laughter. They were four years old and named Alex and Caroline after Emlin's siblings.

"How about this?" Sean fit one end of a strand in his mouth, held the other between his fingers, and inhaled it noisily, the sauce splattering his cheeks. *Baby bird*, Jane thought.

The twins laughed so hard they stopped making any sounds; their small bodies shook uncontrollably as they laughed and laughed and couldn't catch their breath.

"Ow," Caroline wailed finally, pressing her stomach. "I can't breathe!"

"Stop it," Jane told Sean.

"Try and make me." Sean put the tip of another strand between his lips and turned toward the twins.

"Enough," Emlin said, "let's all calm down now. Sean, eat that normally."

"Oh, don't be a spoilsport." Via's *S*'s sloshed in her mouth. "They're just enjoying themselves. Is that so wrong?" She gave a small, bitter grunt, then looked down at her plate. Her head bobbed as it hung forward, slack. There were two cigarettes stubbed into her food.

Emlin considered what to do. He was as wary as Jane when Via was like this.

"Please," Caroline said.

"Sean," Jane pleaded.

Emlin found his authority. "All right, all right. Sean, stop or you'll be sorry."

Sean leaned over his plate and let the strand fall. Jane looked sideways at her mother. To her surprise, Via merely shrugged and touched her glass for a refill. Francis had the bottle in front of him. He looked at Emlin.

"What are you asking his permission for? I'm your sister." Via pushed her glass his way.

Emlin didn't object. He'd performed open-heart surgery on the Australian teenager the day before and hadn't arrived home until three in the morning. Eighteen hours standing in one place, and then back at work again before eight to check on his patients. He was exhausted.

"Perhaps we should wait a bit," Francis suggested. "We could have coffee and brandy later."

"Or we could do both. You're the one who said we were going to have fun tonight."

"That I did." He made a show of wrapping his napkin around the bottle before he poured, and the twins laughed again. Via's drink was red now, rather than brown. Jane knew Susan had tasted wine, but she herself wasn't allowed, or so Via had decreed once, when Sean had grabbed a glass and swilled the dregs. Most likely, Via would have allowed Jane to try it had she asked at the right moment, but Jane never asked again. She was a child who wasn't allowed even a sip of wine, because wine wasn't for children. The restriction was holy; her mother had made the rule.

"*I'm* having fun," Sean said.

Everyone looked at him, wanting it to be true. He sensed his moment in the spotlight and made faces. The twins laughed, then Francis, Via, Jane, and finally Emlin. They laughed on top of laughter, egging each other on. Every time it seemed as though the laughter was about to ebb, someone drew a breath and launched in again.

"That Sean," Via said happily. She could change in an instant.

"I know!" Emlin was eager for Via to be this version of herself.

"You see?" Francis said. "I was right. Here's to the Beatles."

"The Beatles!"

"Whoever they are," Emlin teased.

"Don't pay any attention. He's an old fuddy-duddy," Via said. But no one took her seriously.

. . .

Everyone was in the den except Emlin. They were in awe.

"I could be a decorator!" Francis clapped his hands.

He was pleased with the quick transformation he'd made of the room. A row of chairs faced the television, backed by the sofa. He'd covered the bookcases with the serape rug and the television with the throw blankets, which he'd draped and tied to look like velvet curtains. It was a theater.

"I want to keep it this way all the time!" Via whirled around. "It's so inviting, so like—I don't know. Somewhere where people care about art, and ideas."

"I'm not sure we can legitimately call this art," Francis

37

said, pointing at the television. "Or claim there are ideas to be found there."

"You know what I mean. I'm talking about an attitude, a curiosity. Everything that is not Wynnemoor. But I'm not going to think about any of that tonight. Right, children?"

They nodded absentmindedly. They couldn't stop staring at the magical room.

"Now if only we can get through one evening without Emlin going to the hospital."

"I have an idea," said Sean. He walked over to the telephone and took the receiver off the cradle.

Via giggled. "You're awful! We can't do that!" They all looked at her. She giggled again. "Can we?"

It had come to seem implausible that she had once fantasized about a career in science or medicine. She'd also daydreamed of having TB and taking the gold cure in the Swiss Alps, dressed in a thick, snow-bright nightgown. But it was Emlin who'd really had TB, who was really the doctor. She'd become her fantasy's wife.

"It's only for an hour," Sean said.

Via pressed her palms together and brought her fingers to her lips. "This is a plan, isn't it?" she said to Francis.

Jane couldn't stand it. She cupped the receiver in her palm like a broken bird and lifted it back onto the cradle. "The patients," she said matter-of-factly.

Via looked at her, her firstborn, the child who'd ended her own childhood, a child in whom she couldn't recognize any feature as her own, who was becoming more and more unfamiliar. Yet she had an awful feeling that to Jane she was transparent.

"Yes, Jane. The patients. When you're right, you're right." She walked to the window and stared out.

"Oh, come on, Jane," Sean said. "You always ruin everything." He banged his fist against the top of the sofa.

"Now that," Francis said to Jane, "is an example of hyperbole. A gross exaggeration. As a writer, you need to know these terms." He tapped her shoulder just the way Grand did. He was trying to comfort her. She felt a polite gratitude for his effort, but it was mostly a reflex. The greater part of her was ripped with doubt. She knew she wasn't wrong, but why didn't they? It was an old mystery, one she'd tried to solve many times. Francis saw her suffering, and considered what it would take for her to find relief: growing up and leaving.

Francis sniffed the air. "Does anyone smell popcorn?"

The children cheered. Even Jane smiled when Emlin came in carrying a large green bowl domed with buttered corn.

"My hero," Via said, spreading her arms.

Emlin looked at her intently. Whatever he saw in her face made him plunk the bowl unceremoniously on the side table and go to where she stood. He put his hands on her waist and she grabbed a hunk of his sweater and twisted it, pulling him toward her.

"Am I really your hero?"

"Maybe. I'll tell you later. If you're here."

"Is that a promise?" His voice was gruff. Different.

"I said, maybe."

"Two minutes!" Francis flicked the lights. "Everyone take your seats."

"I call I'm holding the popcorn," Sean said.

Caroline objected, on the grounds that Sean wouldn't share. Francis rushed to get extra bowls from the kitchen so they could divide the booty fairly. Emlin and Via began to dance the way they danced at weddings, swaying from foot to foot, their bodies close, her right arm and his left bent up between them. When they kissed, Jane took her seat.

VIA AND EMLIN HAD MET at the hospital where
Emlin had been on staff for eight years. Via was a college girl
volunteering as a candy striper and Emlin was recovering
from TB that he'd picked up while working as a M.A.S.H.
doctor in Korea. Via was rounder then, and full of the confidence of a girl who liked boys and never doubted that they
liked her back, a girl whose father always told her she was the
most beautiful female in any room into which she walked.
She was not intimidated by the handsome doctor lying in
room 1342, bed B. Because she had accomplished nothing in
her life, she believed herself to be his equal. She flirted with
him—what was the danger?—and he flirted back, to the fur-
thest extent of his strength. Not surprisingly, he began to
feel better rapidly after they met. He wanted to be up and
around way before his doctors allowed him. Perhaps if he
had, the romance would have run a swift course and ended
up in Via's history as the episode of the Dalliance with an
Older Man. As it was, they had time to grow attached before
he returned to his regular hectic schedule, time that otherwise would never have materialized for them to fall in love.

Via knew he adored her and wasn't surprised when, during a walk on the campus across the street from the hospital, he asked her to marry him. What surprised her was how happy she was after she'd said yes.

From Nonny and Grand's point of view, Emlin was a poor choice. He wasn't from around. He was thirty-five. He'd had a disease, a dirty disease that had crippled and killed dozens of people in the poor neighborhood where Grand grew up. Worst of all, in their view, was that he had a job that was a marriage. If Via didn't know it, they did; they had friends who were doctors and had seen the strain it put on their families. They predicted disaster if Via went through with her plans to marry him. Nonny tried to tell her that once Emlin was back on his feet he wouldn't be spending all day every day with her anymore. Via brushed this off, impatient with being told the obvious. It excited her to defy them. When they realized she was "serious" about him, they plotted to change her mind. Grand offered her a tour of Europe, but she told them to save their money for her honeymoon. Next, they asked Francis to introduce her to some of his friends in New York; no one had yet admitted aloud that Francis's friends would hardly provide an adequate counter-gravitational pull on Via. Finally, Nonny took her for lunch at the club and told Via, after nervously asking for saltines with her vichyssoise, that all she wanted was a happy life for her children, which could much more easily be had in Via's case in the company of a less complicated man than Emlin MacLeod. Billy Price, for instance, who dropped in to pay his respects to Nonny and Grand whenever he was home from Princeton. Nonny suggested they invite Billy down for a weekend at the shore, and made the further, awkward suggestion that her father would be very generous if Via married someone like him. Far more subtle, yet unmistakably there, was the implication that there would be no such largesse if Via persisted in knotting herself to the one-lunged doctor from Florida.

Via folded her napkin and set her knife and fork at four o' clock. "I wonder which is worse? Having a dirty disease? Or doing dirty work."

She walked out of the dining room through the porch doors and saw the splendor of the grass tennis courts as a slaving field, where she'd once been a field hand. She went directly to the train station, then to the hospital, where she woke Emlin with a new, more lascivious kind of kiss.

For their part, Emlin's parents, soft-spoken but shrewd Floridians, fretted about the liberal Northern attitudes toward race relations and advised Emlin to check Via's ancestry very carefully. "Can you be sure your children would be white?" his mother wrote to Emlin in a clawing, spidery hand. Via laughed when he told her, but it bothered her. Because Grand had been poor when he was young, she felt she had to go further to prove herself than did her friends who seemed to have inherited leeway as a birthright from the Social Register.

"Little does she know that we'd have more beautiful babies than anybody," she exclaimed.

Via was always forthright with Emlin, to the point of

naïveté. If she'd been more calculating, or more experienced, she'd have known it was foolish to be so sure of herself, not to mention that she might have seen him more clearly, and as less of an answer.

Olivia Gordon became Olivia MacLeod, a wife, and then a housewife, and then a mother. When they were first married, she and Emlin lived in an apartment in the city near the hospital in West Philadelphia, and even when she was weighed down with the burden of Jane not-yet-walking and baby Sean and bags of food and two flights of stairs to climb, she felt unfettered there. Emlin was the one who wanted to move to Wynnemoor. He couldn't imagine a city childhood for Jane and Sean and whoever else might come along. He grew up in Palatka, Florida, and ran free along the river for his entire boyhood.

The MacLeods lived part way down Willow Lane, in a brick house inset with fieldstones, black shutters, and the bright red door that Via had painted with coat after coat until it shone like lacquer. Grand had helped Emlin buy the house (after all) on the assumption that Emlin was good for the loan, considering his future earnings. It was only half a mile from the Gordons' house. Once, when the MacLeods lost power in a snowstorm, Via put the younger children on a sled, and she and Jane pulled them over to her parents' house where Nonny made them hot chocolate and they huddled by the fire while Grand told them ghost stories. Then Nonny brought Via's old debutante dresses down from the attic, and Via, Jane and Caroline put them on and whirled around the living room, spinning and then sitting down abruptly so their skirts encircled them. Mostly, however, Via regretted living so close to her parents.

Emlin went back to work after the wedding. Nonny and Grand had been right about his hours; he worked around the clock, operating, teaching, writing papers, conducting experiments. He didn't know how to work and be present at home in the course of the same day. Either he was working or not. He and Via conceived all their children in the summer when they stayed at the Gordons' breezy shore cottage. Jane and the twins were born in April, nine months from July 4th weekend. They created Sean over Labor Day, so he arrived in early June. Emlin attended their births, but on every other birthday, at some point during the party, the phone would ring and ten minutes later he'd be on the expressway, speeding toward the hospital. Supposedly, he'd been there when Sean blew out three candles, including one to grow on, but none of the children could remember it. They saw him so seldom that they felt shy when they did. Via was with them, one of them in many ways. He was an adult from another world.

In the afternoons Via was liable to pack the children into the station wagon and take them over to visit one of her friends or another, so the mothers could commiserate while the children wandered around, watched but not seen. Via's friends were women like her, young women with large pretty houses and small pretty children and husbands whom they didn't see as much as they'd imagined they might when they agreed to marry. The men were hunters who came back at night with their kill and left in the morning to track down more. The women were shocked to have gone from being carefree college girls with lots of dates and friends to the loneliness of marriage. They'd seen their mothers live the very same lives, but they'd seemed older, and different. They also saw other women their age who weren't bothered by the arrangement. Via knew girls from school who'd turned out like that, accepting and content. They were happy with the division of labor, happy to run their houses and their children with the money their husbands got elsewhere.

Via tried periodically to feel that way, but it never lasted. A few years later, when the women's liberation movement swung through everyone's consciousness, she championed the idea of work and women getting out of the house, but in truth she'd have been more gratified by having her husband in the nest, with nobody going anywhere.

. . .

To prevent any funny business, Jane positioned herself between Sean and the twins. Emlin pulled his chair close to Via's. When Jane turned around to make a comment, she saw they were holding hands. She smiled and they smiled back. Out of the corner of her eye she thought she saw something else, something odd and out of place, but when she looked again she couldn't find it, and guessed it must have been nothing.

Francis tapped Jane on the shoulder. "We have a really big shoe for you tonight." He handed her his loafer.

"I can beat that!" Emlin tossed his slipper into her lap. He and Via were flushed and a little wild. Their mood made the children float.

"Shoe me some more," Sean said. He was a clever child, the most precocious of the four.

Jane held her feet up, displaying her Indian moccasins. The twins raised their legs, copying her.

Ed Sullivan mentioned the Beatles and the audience screamed. The children looked at each other, amazed. They began to bounce up and down.

None of them paid much attention during the other acts. In that way it wasn't like a theater after all.

"This is a relief," Emlin said.

The adults were somber now. They were thinking of the president and how he'd been murdered a few months earlier. Via had bitten at her thumbs watching the caisson drag forward and was still biting at them months later. All winter they'd been wary, spotting fragility everywhere. They'd tiptoed through Christmas. The gates at the stubs of their U-shaped drive hadn't gotten much use lately. Emlin had had men come to install the gates so the children could ride their bikes freely, shorn of the potential to drift accidentally into the street when Via's back was turned for just a sec; or perhaps even when she was watching; with four children one might drift away even when she was right there, it only took an instant, things happened; even presidents got shot. Now the gates stood open, but not because Emlin and Via had become more lax; if anything, it was the opposite. They were more cautious than ever, more jumpy and anxious. Last year the children had been allowed outside by themselves to build snowmen and waddle like robots around the back yard in their stiff snowsuits; this year Emlin had declared Via had to be with them when they went out, unless they were on the terrace. She didn't like the snow, so they didn't go out much, except when they played in cranky confinement right by the house.

Jane imagined what it was like for John-John and Caroline, who reminded her of the twins. People said they were too young to understand, but she wasn't sure.

"Ssshh!" Francis raised his arms like a conductor. "Everyone, be quiet!"

The Beatles appeared. They blinked at the bright studio lights, and smiled bashfully as the audience shrieked. Jane leaned forward.

"What in God's name are they wearing? Where's the leather?" Francis bellowed, and Via shushed him.

The boys began to play.

"That's John," Sean said, touching the screen.

"No, I think that's Paul," said Uncle Francis.

As they discussed this point, Jane turned around to look at her parents. Via rolled her eyes, showing how silly she thought they were, Francis and Sean; they should just be enjoying things. She was curled up against Emlin, taking for granted that he would accept her weight, the pressure of her head on his shoulder and her arm against his, her knees bent to the side and propped on his leg. She looked as though she would have crawled into him if it were possible. He smiled at Jane, and lifted his hand onto her mother's knee.

"Watch," he told her. He was sensitive to her, and considerate, but often unclear about what she needed most.

She did as he told her and turned back to the screen.

. . .

The children were put to bed shortly afterward. Via was strict about bedtime—*my shift ends at seven-thirty*—and exceptions such as this one extended no further than necessary.

Sean and Jane usually talked or played a game until Sean drifted off.

"How about Ghost?" he suggested.

"No," Jane said. "Not tonight." She wanted to think about the Beatles. There'd been a shift inside her as she watched them. She saw in them what she felt in herself. She'd thought she alone felt it. But there they were—pining.

"You're no fun," Sean said.

It was the same thing Via said to Emlin. Jane didn't think it true of either of them.

THE BEDROOM DOOR opened, and Emlin streaked through the hall, one hand pushing the tails of a white shirt into his pants, the other dangling his shoes, his fingers hooked over their stiff tongues. Francis stepped back into the dark.

Jane followed Emlin down the stairs, her heart rushing. "Daddy, what's wrong?"

He turned his head and talked over his shoulder. "I have to get to the hospital." He groped for the switch and flicked it. Jane blinked against the sudden light, anxious to see his expression.

"Is there an emergency? With that Australian girl?" She took his shoes from him and placed them in front of the bench.

"I don't know. The phone's dead. I'm going in to make sure nothing's wrong." He stroked his forehead with his thumb and forefinger and shook his head.

She went to the closet for his coat and brought it to him. He reached for his overshoes and sat down.

"Thanks, Misses. You should go back to bed."

"Uh-huh." But she didn't leave. Instead she watched him ready himself, the way she had a hundred times, so often that he behaved the way he would were he alone. He crooked his elbows and turned his wrists over, his fingers bent loosely toward his palms, as he buttoned his cuffs. He bent over his shoes and pulled the leather laces up straight, measuring the tips to each other until they were even, then tied and looped them in one knot and then another. Even when in a hurry, he was precise. Jane loved him so much she didn't know how she bore it. The sight of him getting dressed made her chest ache.

A thought occurred to her. She walked into the den.

The stairs cracked, and Via's rings scraped the bannister. She didn't see Jane, but walked straight over to Emlin. Her thin silky nightgown left her arms bare, and she rubbed them as she watched him tie his tie. "You're not really going in, are you?"

He looked up at her. "I have to. They may have been calling me all night."

"But they'll call someone else. If they can't reach you?"

"If there's a problem with one of my patients"—he stood and shook the legs of his pants over the tops of his shoes—"I want to be there."

Via struggled to stay calm. "You'll be there in the morning. It's only a few more hours."

Jane walked carefully across the den. Her eyes adjusted to the faint light from the hall. The furniture had been returned to normal, but she could still smell popcorn and Via's Joy.

She walked to the telephone and felt the empty slot of the

cradle. With quick, excited fingers she groped down the side of the phone to the cord and followed it as it pulled over the lip of the table and down to the floor. A pillow covered the receiver. She lifted it and heard the droning dial tone.

"Hey," she called, "guess what?" She jumped up and turned on the table lamp to show what she'd found.

Via came to the door. "What are you doing up?" She hugged herself.

"The phone's not dead!"

Emlin appeared in the doorway. "What do you mean?"

"It was just off the hook. Like this."

He barged past Via, who grabbed at the wall as if she were in danger of falling. He didn't apologize, however, but crossed straight to the table where Jane showed him what she'd found. "It's not dead. You can call the hospital. Maybe you don't have to go."

He hung up the phone and lifted it again. "I'll be damned," he whispered.

Jane glanced shyly at Via. To her surprise, Via looked angry.

Emlin dialed the hospital. "How did you know?" he asked Jane.

"I saw it—"

He held up his hand for her to wait. "Yes, this is Dr. MacLeod. Put me through to the floor."

"Jane. Go to bed," Via said sharply. She was shivering.

Emlin placed his hand over the receiver. "Just a minute. I want to know—Yes, it's Dr. MacLeod. Everything all right? Uh-huh. How's the Emerson girl?" He patted Jane on the shoulder. Jane heard the nurse on the other end of the line read him numbers. "That's a little high," he said, mainly to himself. Another pause.

"Jane," Via hissed, beckoning with one hand and pointing toward the stairs with the other.

Jane cocked her head, confused.

"All right. No, I'm coming in. That temp concerns me." Emlin hung up and put his hands on his hips, his expression both thoughtful and eager. Jane had seen him this way at the hospital as he stopped to speak with interns and other doctors along the glary corridors. He looked at Via. Her fingers had curled into fists and her jaw was tight. He closed his eyes, as if he were very tired, so tired he could go to sleep standing up, tired of everything, tired in a way that couldn't be made up for by his freshly starched shirt or his helpful child or the fact that he routinely saved lives.

Jane reached for his hand. He pressed his thumb into her palm and swung it gently, tapping the paw they formed together against his side.

"So how'd you say you figured that out?" He yawned, sucking in a mouthful of air.

"I don't know. I think I saw it off the hook before."

"Before? When?"

"It must have happened when we put the furniture back," Via said. "Come on, Jane."

"No." Jane shook her head. She was trying hard to remember. "Before then." She rubbed one cold foot on top of the other, like a cricket.

"That's strange." Emlin wiggled her hand again and let

go. He began to walk back to the hall, toward his coat, but Via stepped into the doorway, blocking his way.

"No!" she growled.

Jane was so surprised she laughed.

"Olivia—"

"I mean it, Emlin. If you leave this house tonight, I won't be here when you come back."

He thrust his hands into his pockets. For a moment the room felt charged, like air heavy with rain and electricity. Then in the same instant that Jane remembered seeing the phone off the hook during the show, seeing but not understanding, Emlin looked at his wife and said, "You."

Via's head jerked back as if she'd been slapped. "Me? Don't be ridiculous." She crossed her arms and stood up straight, but she was nervous.

Emlin strode forward and, when she held her ground, shoved her aside with the back of his arm as if she were a sapling blocking a trail. She banged against the wall, harder than she'd been pushed. Too hard, Jane thought dispassionately. Via followed Emlin to the door. "How can you accuse me of such a thing?"

He pulled on his boots. He curved a scarf around his neck.

Via paced. "I don't know how it happened. Maybe one of the children did it. Jane, you were playing with it, weren't you?"

Her father looked at Jane. She was too shocked to speak.

"I've got to go." Emlin opened the door.

"Wait!" Via grabbed him. When he stopped, when he did

as she said and waited, when he wanted to be convinced, she loosened her grip and rested her hands against his chest. "Please."

Emlin looked out into the dark. The cold threaded past him in iced ribbons. Jane heard a door close upstairs.

"Don't go." Via spoke in a low, husky, insinuating tone. She was promising something.

Emlin hung his head. For a moment it seemed as though he might come back in. He listed toward the comfort of oblivion. He rocked on his feet as he considered. Finally, he raised his eyes to hers. "What I can't seem to make you understand is that you have me."

"Make me understand," Via coaxed. "Show me."

He brushed her hair off her cheek and traced her eyebrow with his finger. "If only you could be a little patient. She could have died, you know."

"But she didn't. And maybe I should be a little patient. Then I'd see you."

He grimaced and dropped his hand. He'd been in the cold long enough for his breath to turn cloudy. "I'll probably stay in at this point. I have a surgery at eight."

Via understood she'd lost. She stepped backward, breaking contact. She grew stiff and shrill. "You think I was joking? I can't take it anymore. You leave now and I won't be here when you get home."

"Well," he said, jangling his keys. "That's too bad."

He turned toward the night, and Jane felt a horrible stab in her side, cutting her apart. "I'm going with you, Daddy!"

55

Via grabbed her arm as she ran for Emlin. "No! You come back upstairs!"

"Please, Mummy, please," Jane whimpered.

"Let go of her," Emlin said coldly. "Now."

"Don't think I don't mean it. I'm leaving," Via said. She pushed Jane toward him. The door slammed shut.

Jane stepped onto the frozen flagstones. Emlin lifted her and she wrapped her legs around his waist. He smelled of cold tweed and, faintly, the sea.

She began to sob. "It's okay," he said, fumbling her hair. "It's okay. You stay here and go back to sleep."

He carried her back inside. The hall was empty, Via gone.

"Don't go." Her voice was husky with fear.

He began to peel her arms from his neck.

"I took the phone off the hook. It was me," she said frantically. "So don't be mad at Mummy." She wanted it to be true so badly that she began to believe it.

"Oh, Jane," he said. "You know too much."

She clung to him hard as he continued to unwrap her, but when she realized it was no use, she let him help her slide down the length of his body until her feet touched the rug. She allowed him to let go of her and stood alone. She was helpless.

"Don't miss me," he said. "I'm always with you. You understand that, don't you?"

To please him she nodded.

"I wish your mother did," he said quietly. He rubbed her shoulder. "Go to sleep. Sean will be up soon."

She made herself look up at him. He winked. She ran to

the living room window and stepped in front of the heavy damask draperies to watch him drive away.

. . .

All the lights were on upstairs, including the one in Jane's room. She stood on the top step, wondering what was going on.

Her mother came out of Francis's room. "Hurry up! Get some clothes together!"

"Why?" She was frightened by Via's wild energy.

"Because. I can't live like this!" The words trailed over her shoulder as Via strode down the hall. She went into the twins' room.

Sean had a pile of models on his bed. He began stuffing them into a pillow case.

"What's happening?" Jane asked.

"We're going to Nonny and Grand's." He shrugged. "I guess we have no heat again."

Jane pressed her hand to the radiator. It was warm.

. . .

There were no other cars on the road. The ride took ten minutes, but the twins nodded off and had to be carried inside.

The kitchen looked different with Nonny and Grand in Florida. It was just a cold, dusty room.

"Come on, Via," Francis said. "You've proved your point. Let's go back. It's freezing in here."

"How have I proved my point, if he doesn't even know I'm

57

here yet? And don't be such a sissy. It'll warm up. Go downstairs and light the boiler."

"I don't know how to do that. And I don't want to. That's
why I live in an apartment. And I am a sissy, by the way."

Via tightened her jaw. "All right, I'll do it. Get them in
bed."

Jane carried Alex. The stairs crackled under her feet like
twigs in the woods. She remembered Francis telling a story
about memorizing the creaks so he could avoid them when
he wanted to sneak out at night.

She thought, *we are sneaking in*.

. . .

Jane had a room to herself, the small room off Via's childhood bedroom that Nonny used for sewing. Jane had always
wanted to sleep in the white iron daybed, but not now.

She lay awake. The pipes banged as they warmed, startling
her. The air smelled of Nonny's skin. Angus snuffled at the
foot of her bed.

She'd brought her book and her notebook. She opened
them and made herself read for she couldn't bear thinking
about Emlin; it was horrible that he didn't know where they
were. By morning she still hadn't found the page she remembered liking so much. Instead, she found a peculiar line that
she read four times.

Dear Reader, I loved him.

She closed the book. She looked at the title on the cover,
same as her own name, until the letters blurred and became
unintelligible.

She listened to the noises of the house, the creaking stairs, the doors, the footsteps, until Uncle Francis came in to tell her it was a snow day. "No school, no school!" He was as jubilant as if the news applied to him. Jane realized: *he's thinking of England.* "Your mother's making pancakes!" He saw Jane's expression and frowned. "But you wanted to go to school today, didn't you? The author was coming. That's too bad. Who was it, anyway?"

"I don't know the name." Jane shrugged, her thin shoulders lifting above the heavy satin quilt. "It's okay."

"How about later you show me your book?"

"Maybe."

"Good. It's a date. See you downstairs?"

"I'm not hungry right now."

He hesitated. She could tell he was trying to decide what to say.

"It's going to be all right," she told him. "We'll be going back soon."

He nodded vigorously. "See you in a bit."

When she was alone again, she opened the "The Happy MacMillans." She looked at the picture she'd drawn of them when they walked in to find their house burglarized. They had their hands pressed to their cheeks, and their mouths were dark, horrified circles. She closed the notebook, lay on her side facing the wall, and began to wait.

1979

THERE ARE SPIES everywhere," the man said to his companion in a stage whisper. He pointed behind his hand, yet without concealment, at Jane, who was browsing a few feet away in the Tower of London gift shop.

Embarrassed, she stumbled backward and bumped against a wall of postcards. The man winked at her, which made her blush even more. He was about her age, and noticeably good-looking. A tall woman accompanied him. She was striking, too, with dark rings painted around her eyes and spiky platinum hair. They were glamorous, and looked wildly anomalous among the toy beefeaters and piles of picture books and cases of miniature spoons. There was no chance of Jane slipping away, although her old self longed to do exactly that. Her new self, though, wanted to see what would happen next.

"I'm sorry for staring, but I thought I saw a ghost a moment ago," she explained. Immediately, she felt she'd said both too much and too little; she'd made no sense. She was out of practice in talking to people.

"We live to be stared at. Please, feel free."

Jane laughed. The man grinned along with her, and nodded as if approving the nature of the exchange.

"I'm Nigel Kirby-Kerr, and this is Colette Rey. We came here today to case the crown jewels. I must admit, however, that we're feeling discouraged by the Tower's fortification." He sighed with mock despair. "I think we've ruled out jewel thief as a career option."

Colette wrapped herself around his arm. "You have a career. You're a novelist."

Jane noticed that the backs of her hands were scarred.

"Hardly," Nigel said, and quickly switched the topic. "So who are you, and what's your excuse for being here?"

Jane introduced herself and said she was a tourist.

"Ah. Too bad. So you'll be leaving soon?"

"Not really. I have a flat. I'm planning to stay a year. But I think of myself as a tourist when I come to places like this."

"You're not ashamed to be a tourist? Most Americans want to appear to be natives."

She shook her head. "I'd be ashamed to pretend I was anything else." She displayed her *Blue Guide*.

"Bravo," said Nigel. "And you haven't developed an accent either."

"I don't have a policy against it," Jane said. She'd given this question some thought; she'd had to, as it was difficult not to pick up the vocabulary and cadences that swirled around her in the shops and the streets. Were English accents pretentious, if one wasn't English? She decided the issue had to be treated on a case-by-case basis. For herself the case was clear-cut. "I just don't think I could pull it off."

"You sound perfect the way you are," Nigel said. "Doesn't she?"

"Yes, she does."

Jane was surprised that Colette was American; she seemed too chic. Her delight at their common nationality prompted another surprise. For weeks, she'd been so absorbed in discovering the city that she hadn't known she'd been lonely.

"I wouldn't say that," she mumbled. "Anyway." She ran her thumb beneath the strap of her shoulder bag, a standard gesture of departure, affording them an easy getaway. But Nigel continued to gaze at her with an expression of triumph, as if she were the very thing he'd hoped to find in this store. It's just charm, she told herself. He's one of those people who knows how to make you feel singled out; but it worked on her anyway.

"We have to be off now, but we'll be at home on Saturday at four. Why don't you come by?" Colette said.

"You must," Nigel agreed. He reached into his inside jacket pocket and pulled out a card and a pen and wrote, using his palm as a desk. "Here's the address. It's in Hampstead."

Jane took it and admired his graceful handwriting. "I live in Belsize Park," she said.

"A stone's throw. Could destiny be at play here?"

"I tend to think of destiny as being at *work*."

He frowned with sardonic concern. "Puritan ancestry?"

Jane grimaced back at him. She was having fun. "More or less."

"I'm so sorry. We did such a smart thing in getting rid of those people. But come on Saturday and we'll see what we can do about that. Exorcising the past is our specialty."

"I'll look forward to it," she said, and held out her hand. She wasn't in the habit of shaking the hands of people her own age, but the occasion seemed to call for it. Colette, however, scowled at the formality, and leaned in for an embrace.

"I feel like we know each other already," she said close to Jane's ear. "We're going to be great friends, I can sense it."

Jane inhaled her scents. Perfume. Powder. Cigarettes. In spite of her exotic appearance, there was a stirring familiarity about her. Jane didn't need much encouragement to agree. Awkwardly, but with honest feeling, she hugged Colette back.

That night, after leaving crumbs on the counter for the field mouse with whom she shared the flat, Jane sat down at the small table by the window to make her daily entry in her five-year diary. She devoted all of the space to her new acquaintances, soberly tempering her excitement at the prospect of friendship with the observation that they were like Fitzgerald characters and the conjecture that they probably approached strangers all the time. She wrote nothing about seeing Emlin's ghost that afternoon at the end of a stony corridor; there was no point mentioning it when it had just been the Tower, playing tricks. *Anyway*, she thought as she pulled back her neat covers and slid down the cool sheets, *ghosts can't travel across water.*

. . .

From studying her *London AZ*, she guessed it was about two kilometers from her bedsit in Primrose Gardens up to Nigel and Colette's house and, not wanting to be late, she gave herself an hour to cover the ground. She'd walked on Hampstead Heath before, but had never gone up as far as their neighborhood. That people were expecting her gave the walk a different quality. When she studied the houses, she noticed bicycles, flowerpots, and books on the windowsills rather than the architecture. The bottle of wine she'd brought as a present was a welcome weight in her backpack. She wasn't a mere tourist anymore.

She rang their bell at precisely the hour. Her public life had been based on the punctuality of school; it wouldn't have occurred to her to calculate what might pass for being fashionably late.

"It's open!"

Carefully, she turned the knob and walked into a large foyer. It surprised her that people around her age had a whole house to themselves. Colette and Nigel seemed to have passed into adulthood.

From where she stood she could see three rooms, all painted differently; a pale lilac in the entrance hall where she stood, and pink and mint in the parlor rooms on either side. Jordan Almonds, she thought. The bands of molding on the walls were white, as were the ceilings. It was a Victorian house, but there was no dark wood anywhere. She'd assumed the insides of the houses she passed by everyday were much like the museums, dark and stately. She immediately liked this style very much.

"In here!"

She followed the voice into the pink living room. Nigel Kirby-Kerr stood at a table by the front window, arranging something in front of him.

"Hello," she said.

He craned around. "Oh, Jane. One second. Have a look around." He turned back to his task.

She was happy to be treated so casually. She slipped her knapsack off her shoulders and sat it near the wall. On her tour she saw a deep purple dining room with casement windows that opened onto a garden and heavy art books stacked along the wainscoting.

"All right. All finished." He came over to give her kisses, tock, tock, back and forth by her cheeks. "You came."

Jane nodded. Had there been any question?

"Good. You're the first. Most people show up a bit later. I'm ready at four, though, just in case anyone decides to be on time."

Most people? How many people were coming? It embarrassed her that she'd believed she was the only one. "I can leave and come back." She pointed at the door.

"Don't you dare. I'm grateful for the company." He slipped his hands into his pants pockets and smiled at her. His looks made her giddy, and she grinned back. He had all the lovely English attributes: slippery brown hair, a thin, elegant mouth, and fair skin that changed hues with his mood. Purposeful good breeding in the flesh. She wanted him to stop looking at her.

"What were you making?" she asked.

It worked. He glanced at the table.

"Oh. That old thing. That's how I killed time this afternoon."

When they walked closer, she saw the construction was not merely an aesthetic arrangement—he'd used branches, leaves, mosses, twigs, stones—but that the items formed a little town, a fairy town. There were no figures present, but he'd created a strong sense of habitation, as if everyone—a fairy court—had just stepped away for a moment.

"You made this? It's incredible."

"I have to do something while I'm waiting. Colette's upstairs getting dressed. That starts at about two. She leaves me rattling around down here on my own for hours. There's only so much time I can devote to setting up glasses and crisps."

"I didn't realize this was a party. I'm afraid I'm underdressed." Jane had on a pair of jeans, black Chucks, and an old cashmere sweater of her grandmother's, green with flowers beaded across the chest. As always, she wore her hair in a braid pulled forward and hanging down her front.

"Not at all. Americans should always wear blue jeans." He crossed his arms. "You don't know what an 'at home' is, do you?"

She shook her head. "Sorry."

"I'm the one who's sorry. I didn't think."

He explained the English custom of sending out cards saying you'd be at home every week at a specific hour. Then anyone who chose to was free to drop by. It was a party without a guest list.

Jane liked the idea, but couldn't imagine how to plan for it. "Does it ever happen that nobody comes?"

"It doesn't happen here." He sounded unsure of whether or not he was happy about that. It was the first glimpse she'd had of him beneath the polished surface. "And you look terrific, by the way."

"Thanks." Nonny had taught her to accept a compliment, whether or not she agreed.

"You're going to see a lot of purple hair today."

"I think I can handle it."

"*You* wouldn't color your hair, though."

He was sure of himself, cocksure. She couldn't let him get away with it. "Why not? It might be fun, for a change."

"Because you wouldn't. I can tell. You don't need to do things like that, because you know who you are."

Was that a compliment, too? Another statement she should graciously accept? She more than disputed it; it simply wasn't true. But should she inform Nigel? Chances were, he was just being charming again.

"I should hope so," she said. She was pleased with this reply; it seemed both honest and polite—and witty, too.

He didn't laugh. "I wish—" he began, but was abruptly interrupted by a shout from above. *He wishes what*, Jane wondered. He seemed to have everything.

"What's going on?"

"Jane's here. From the Tower!" Nigel shouted back.

"Oh good. I'll be right down," Colette said. "Stop talking. I don't want to miss anything."

"Okay!" he called. Then he winked at Jane. "Don't hold your breath."

"I did come too early."

"Four is four."

"Let me help you get ready."

"There's nothing to do. People will bring bottles, and Colette likes to make food with company around."

There was a pause. Jane felt awkward in the lull and pressured to fill it, although the pressure wasn't coming from Nigel. "I brought a bottle, too." She retrieved her knapsack.

"Thank you. Will you have some now?"

"No, thanks," she said, automatically following another of Nonny's rules—no drinking before five.

He carried the bottle to a sideboard and set it near the glasses, moving it a quarter of an inch in various directions until he was pleased with how it looked.

She thought of a topic. "I'd love to hear about your book."

"What book?"

She was confused. "I thought Colette said you're a novelist."

"She did, didn't she? I must tell her to stop doing that. It's way ahead of the truth. The most I care to claim is that I'm trying to learn to write, and if I had my way, I'd keep that a secret."

"Trying to learn," she repeated. "I've never heard anyone put it that way before."

"I've never heard anyone who lives here calling herself a tourist."

She smiled, but went on with her thought. "It sounds old-fashioned. As if you were an apprentice."

"Do you write?"

She shook her head. "I did as a child, but I stopped, except for school assignments."

"I began at fifteen. I wrote sonnets."

"In the dead of night, I assume."

"By candlelight."

"I once wrote a poem I liked."

"You should start again. Sorry—let me rephrase. I hate the word 'should,' don't you? What I mean is, why not try it? For fun."

"I don't know . . ."

"Someone has to do it. You're someone, aren't you? Just try one poem."

"One. All right."

"A day," he added.

"No, I only agreed to—"

"Agreed to what?" Colette called.

They walked back to the hall and watched her grand entrance. She made an unusual chatelaine in a pair of paper pants and a tee shirt ripped to shreds, then put back together again with safety pins and electrical tape. She wore moccasins, and thin silver earrings the circumference of a saucer.

72

Her short platinum hair had been brushed severely close to her head, yet the effect was delicate and feminine. A punk princess. As she drew closer to Jane, she smiled broadly and spread her arms; her glass bracelets clinked.

"I knew it! I knew you'd come," she said. Like Nigel, she tocked Jane on both cheeks. "I've been looking forward to it all week."

"I'm happy to be here."

There was a knock on the door. Colette made a face. "We'll talk later. It's show time."

. . .

By six the downstairs rooms were full, and wisps of smoke floated in broken circles up to the ceiling. Jane wondered how much longer she could smile; her jaw ached. She'd had beer spilled on one arm and her toes stepped on numerous times but people smiled at her and made her feel welcome. She was grateful to each one of them; she didn't realize that the world's predisposition toward good-looking girls had come to apply to her.

Colette appeared beside her holding a tray of tiny quiches. "Who are all these people, anyway?" She shrugged happily and disappeared into the copse of bodies that thronged the living room.

Jane didn't recognize most of the music that blared from the speakers. There was a genre new to her that she found appealing, horns over an even beat, which someone told her was called ska. She did know "Wuthering Heights" by Kate

Bush; it yearned out of pub windows as she walked past. And she knew "Roxanne" by the Police, but not much else. She decided she was going to buy a radio.

There were many Americans, various types of Brits, and a few other nationalities strewn in. Jane was asked over and over what she did, a question Nonny had taught her to avoid asking. What if a man has recently lost his job? Or if he's an alcoholic? Jane had accepted the likelihood of these dire scenarios without question, as well as the importance of not calling attention to them. She'd long ago understood the point of manners and reticence, and preferred Nonny's old-fashioned mores to Via's philosophy of unbridled self-expression. It was one of the reasons she picked England when she decided to move away.

Once Nigel was standing next to her when the matter came up. "Jane has a government position she's not at liberty to discuss." He pinched her arm to prevent her from denying it.

"I'm writing a play," the man said, as uninterested in Jane as if she'd been introduced as the maid.

Nigel clapped him on the back. "Super!"

After that, Jane worked up an all-purpose answer about taking the year off. The truth was too complicated to explain. *Think of England*, Via had said when Jane called to announce her plans.

"You always liked that phrase." Via sighed, signifying the great differences between them, the fracturing fact of Jane's admiration for Nonny, the very same woman who'd doomed Via to her bitterness.

74

"That's not why," Jane said.

"And you always had that Beatle thing. Who did you like again?"

"It's not that either."

She wished she could be honest with Via and say, aloud, that she needed to put thousands of miles, a whole gray ocean, between her and her family, so she could figure out who she was apart from them, and what she could do with her life other than trying to make them into the happy family she thought they should be. She wished she could say, too, that she had to get away from reminders of Emlin. Every day during her years at Penn she walked past the hospital where he'd worked. It hadn't helped much to move across the river to Twenty-first Street. He was heavy in her dreams. But the subject of Emlin was more than a taboo for Via. It was extinct.

"All right." Via still gave up quickly. "When are you leaving?"

"Tonight." Nonny and Grand had given her $5,000 for graduation—and as a reward for never starting to smoke—and she had money saved from her summer and college jobs. It was enough to keep her going for a year if she lived simply. That, she believed, she could do.

"That's soon." Via had long before stopped talking to her children about the big decisions in their lives, though she was apt to offer nutritional advice based on articles in the *New York Times*. She and Ned Phelps ate three organic meals every day, no snacks, no desserts. They were lean and looked aristocratic. They lived in a brick Colonial house in Wynnemoor not far from the one with the red door where Jane had spent her childhood—her real house, as she thought of it—and they rented places in the summer in resorts where Ned had friends; Nantucket, Dark Harbor, Bermuda. They had a good life, but Jane had never felt part of it.

"Francis often goes to London on business. He can visit you," Via said.

"That would be nice." Jane meant it. Uncle Francis was an exception to her notion of getting away from her family—as he was an exception to most rules.

"Call me when you have an address?"

"I will."

There was a pause before they hung up. Jane waited, half hoping that her mother might say something. She had no idea what that might be, but it would be significant. She'd had a feeling for a long time that there were unsaid things between them that could change everything.

"Will you be back for Christmas?" Via asked.

A simple, perfunctory question. Not what Jane was waiting for.

"I don't think so."

"Well. Enjoy yourself."

Finally, at the party, Jane was able to apply that remark, but by eight o'clock she was exhausted. She cleared a few glasses into the kitchen and looked for her hostess.

"No, no, no, no, no," Colette shook her finger, "you can't leave yet. We haven't even talked!"

I've been here for four hours, Jane thought. "I have to go."

"Then come back first thing in the morning, okay?"

"What time?"

But Colette was already on her way across the room.

. . .

Nigel was full of bright energy when she arrived at nine. The house, pristine again, smelled of lemon polish, and the curtains, filled with breeze, sailed over the rooms. "Colette said first thing in the morning," Jane told him. "I wasn't sure what that meant."

"She should be down"—he looked at his watch—"any hour now. Morning is rather a personal term for Colette, meaning when she wakes up. Let's make breakfast. You're hungry, aren't you?"

They made toast and eggs in the old kitchen and took two trays out to the patio. The furniture was eclectic, some garden furniture, some not—an Oriental rug that was definitely not. Inside the low wall grew a border of carefully tended plants, the heavy stems staked against embedded branches. Jane recognized dusty miller and begonia. Nigel picked a few yellow and orange flowers off the trailing vines that hung from several large pots and to Jane's surprise ripped the petals onto the eggs.

"Nasturtiums," he said. "They're edible."

Jane didn't want to be rude, or to appear unsophisticated, so she ate what was handed to her without question. As it turned out, she couldn't taste the flowers at all.

Church bells rang. She'd heard them ring every quarter hour during her walk up the hill. English church bells, proclaiming the steadiness of time and God. They steadied her.

77

"I love your house," she said.

"Thank you. Although the credit isn't all mine. It's a let."

Jane stared up at the high dormers. "It looks more cared for than that. The paint colors, the garden . . ."

"Guilty," he said. "I'm a bit of an insomniac. When I can't sleep, I putter."

"You don't write?"

"I probably should, shouldn't I? Oh well." He paused, teapot in hand. "There's that word again. It's hard to get away from, isn't it?" He handed her a cup of tea.

"I wouldn't know where to begin."

"My guess is you have, in coming here."

Jane struggled against her self-consciousness and met his gaze. "Perhaps."

"It's all I think about. Colette, on the other hand, barely knows the meaning of guilt."

Jane wondered if that was the attraction. "How long have you been together?" she asked.

He tipped his head quizzically.

"You and Colette," she clarified.

"For a moment I thought you meant me, as in what a to-gether person I am. You see? I know your American slang."

She smiled. "Not that you don't seem to be—"

"But me and Colette."

She nodded. He frowned, still joking, she thought, but then there was a silence, and she became uncomfortable.

"I'm sorry, it's none of my business." The rules were dif-ferent in England.

"It's all right." He tapped his fingers together lightly. He was slumped in his chair, his feet crossed at the ankle. Jane was aware of his body, his indolent handsomeness. She could see him playing tennis and then flopping down on the grass for a rest. She'd known boys like him in Wynnemoor, boys who could afford to display their torpor. Nigel felt entitled to leisure. "You've asked a perfectly decent question," he said.

"Never mind. I'm really sorry."

"No, no—I want to tell you the truth. I can't say exactly why, but I do. Here's the thing, Jane—I'm gay. As you so cheerfully put it in your great land."

Jane was taken off guard. She'd never before met a gay man who didn't call immediate attention to his homosexuality. Uncle Francis was clear about it, in word and deed. At college the gay boys had dressed vibrantly and spoken a rich, arch dialect that reversed sex roles and conventions in ways meant to shock, or at least attract attention. Nigel displayed no discernible clues with which she was familiar. She'd only noticed his Englishness.

She was unsure of how to respond to his announcement. That's nice? You don't seem it?

She decided to nod and leave it at that.

"You don't mind, do you?" he asked.

"Of course not. My uncle is gay," she offered, and immediately regretted it. "I'm sorry. That was stupid."

"Quite all right. My sister's a girl, if that makes you feel any better."

Jane tried to smile but couldn't manage. "One of the reasons I came to England was because I wanted to live in a place where people behaved. Where they thought before they spoke. Where self-expression was low on the list of desirable qualities. And here I go, blurting away."

"And I wish I lived in America, where I could let it all hang out." Again he spoke the phrase ironically, but he was wistful, and meant it. "I've never actually told anyone before, not directly. It feels rather good."

"I'm glad. But I really am sorry." Why did Colette wear a ring, she wondered?

"I can see that." He kicked playfully at her feet. "You are absolved, although there's no need for it. But tell me about your uncle."

Before she had a chance to answer, there was a small commotion at the back door. A bang. Several curses. Followed by the appearance of an apparition, though a far more worldly one than Emlin MacLeod. Colette clumped down the steps wearing straw slippers and a short turquoise Chinese robe, the sash pulled tight around her narrow waist, over a pair of dotted Swiss pajama pants. She carried a basket. Does she always make entrances, Jane wondered?

Colette yawned as she sat down. "I couldn't sleep."

Nigel and Jane smiled at each other. It was after ten. "Poor baby," Nigel said.

"Tea, please." She patted his arm. Jane noticed the scars on her hands extended up her forearms.

As Nigel prepared her cup, Colette reached in the basket and pulled out a wad of tissues and a jar of Pond's cold cream, and began to remove her makeup. With a practiced swipe she dislodged the sizable grains of dried mascara from her lashes, and then from her face where they'd fallen and formed a dark semicircle on top of her cheekbones. Jane had often read that makeup should be removed before bed, but she kept this information to herself.

Colette stopped her work long enough to take a drink. She looked much younger with her eyes bare. "I have to buy a new coffeemaker. Tea doesn't do it for me."

"Jane was asking about *us*," Nigel said. "So I told her about me."

Colette jerked around to look at him. "Oh?" She replaced her cup in the saucer. Clearly, she hadn't expected this.

"Honestly, you don't owe me any explanations." Jane was flustered. The conversation had gone way beyond the bounds she'd expected. During her walk up to Hampstead earlier, she'd reminded herself not to get her hopes up too high about Nigel and Colette; they had hundreds of friends already. *You're not special*, she told herself. She'd been so convincing that it surprised her now that they seemed to like her as much as she liked them.

"It's not a question of owing," Nigel said. "Is it, Colette?"

"No. I suppose it isn't."

She looked directly at Jane and gave a small laugh and a shrug, as if her initial response had been amusing. Jane followed her lead and shrugged back.

"Only if you want to," Jane said.

"We do. Definitely. You're going to be our great friend, so you should know the truth from the beginning." Colette reached for a piece of toast. "And the first thing you should know, or should I say the second thing"—she paused to take a bite—"is that I'm Nigel's beard."

Colette reached for her cup and took a healthy swig. Her renewed appetite freed Jane to be curious.

"His beard?" She'd never heard the term.

Nigel and Colette exchanged glances. "Our work is cut out for us," Nigel said solemnly.

"No problem." Colette sat back, relaxed and expansive. "We have all day."

. . .

After that Jane often made the trek up to Hampstead, although she never again arrived as early as she had that first morning. Colette and Nigel welcomed her into their lives as if she were a prodigal relative, and she was happy to give up her solitude. She'd thought, during the months she'd spent alone, that she was engaged in a form of asceticism and spiritual exercise; she could be so serious. Looking back, she saw herself as having been in a state of waiting, which she supposed was true of all monastics. Because she wasn't waiting for God, she hadn't recognized it.

What had she been waiting for? Perhaps nothing more than to stop doing so.

Nigel and Colette certainly helped. In a sense, they were permanently at home, their door always open. Colette was an excellent cook, and was most often to be found standing in the kitchen, a Marlboro in one hand and a knife in the other, with a glass of wine nearby.

"It's all in the cutting," she explained to Jane. "Vegetables release their perfumes and flavors when they are cut properly. They are like a woman surrendering to a clever lover. If the knife goes into them the wrong way—" She broke off; the results were unspeakable.

Even though she knew the drill, Jane was always surprised to see Colette slaving over a hot stove. She seemed too modern to place herself there. When Jane pointed out the incongruity, Colette replied that the real liberation of women—of people, for that matter—wasn't an abdication of their traditional roles, but a freedom to pursue what came most naturally. If it was cooking, or running a house, so be it.

"Someone has to make the world beautiful," she said. "I'm committed to doing my part."

Their friends were the happy beneficiaries of this philosophy. Many of them were Americans who'd moved to London to make something of themselves apart from the expectations placed on them back home. The English expected little to nothing from Americans. They were free to go anywhere in the city and to befriend anyone, because there was no place where they belonged.

Painters and poets and novelists came to Nigel and Colette's. Journalists. Editors. Rock-and-roll musicians. Aside from wanting to make something of themselves, what they had in common was the desire to talk. There was an incredible amount of talk on those afternoons and nights, a lot of which Grand would dismiss as hot air. Jane was content to suspend judgment. It was exciting to hear what people wanted to do, all their ideas for creating new things. She'd always been a good listener, a quality that served her well here; her attention to people's plans gave her a reputation for intelligence. At first she was shy about saying she'd started to write poetry, but Colette insisted she be affirmative.

I am Jane MacLeod, a poet from Belsize Park.

No one doubted it, anymore than she doubted what they told her. They were all who they said they were, without a past to impugn their claims. They were free to become the people they wanted to be, if only they dared. Jane was touched by their bravery, and inspired. Each week she found it easier to say what she thought, and to behave with flair.

I wish you could see me, she wrote to Nonny.

I can, Nonny wrote back. *I've always seen you like this.*

Jane began to have a strange sensation, the unfamiliar feeling of liking herself. She didn't tell anyone about that, though, not yet. She didn't want to tempt the Fates. It was enough, for now, to walk into a room full of strangers and believe she had things to offer. To feel she belonged.

. . .

When everyone else had gone—which was apt to be late Saturday night, if not Sunday morning—they continued to trade their histories. All of them wondered about their mothers.

Nigel: She likes her horses more than she does her children.

Colette: She only cared about how I looked.

Jane: I remind her too much of my father.

She told them about Emlin's car accident, and they nodded at her with a knowing, blanketing empathy that proclaimed her situation both awful and par for the course, so that for the first time since she was little—perhaps the first time ever—she didn't feel different. The three of them were each other's ideal siblings, and if in their loyalty they overlooked each other's weaknesses, if their delight in obscure mutual tastes allowed them to ignore larger differences, if in their automatic support they tacitly encouraged unreliable narratives, they honestly meant no harm. They each saw the others as having been harmed enough.

. . .

Nigel was an aristocrat, the eldest son of a solemn man who took notes in the House of Lords while all around him dozed, and a woman who saw the world through a lens of provincial snobbery that kept her sanguine and secure. Nigel grew up in the country, on land so beautiful that even as a small child he understood his luck. If he'd been blind he'd still have been undone by its scents: roses and sweet hay, wet dog and teeming dirt. And it was all to be his.

He didn't know the term for it until he was nine, but his sexuality had also been apparent to him as far back as he could remember. When he read *Confessions of a Mask* by Yukio Mishima, he found in those pages his own experience described; the fascination with the knight rather than the damsel. It was the way he was made, and he'd never questioned it. His parents were furious.

"The one aristocratic family in all of England unwilling to ignore it," he said.

He and Colette met in New York, at a dinner party in the

West Village, where Nigel's sexuality was greeted the opposite from home. Colette thought he was being a fool; if his parents weren't willing to do so, why couldn't he be the one to pretend, if the pretense would reward him with a large chunk of East Sussex? And she knew just the woman to play the part of his intended.

. . .

Getting to know Colette was like learning a branch of the law, for she was strict and had many rules for herself. She wouldn't leave the house in wrinkled clothes or without makeup; she dressed to go to the off-license for cigs. She wouldn't eat without the ceremony of good plates and silver and cloth napkins, even if she was having a couple of crackers for a snack. Nor would she ever under any circumstances wear sweatpants.

"One has to maintain certain standards," she said. "I don't take being an expat as a license to be a slob."

Colette's high habits and her arcane knowledge of pastry dough and linen and sauces had come from her mother, a French war bride whose ambitions had sprung her from a small town near Bourgogne during the Occupation and drove her through a series of husbands until she landed in a ranch house in Pasadena, with a pool and a white Cadillac. She pushed her girls to be on television, but Colette's sister was odd, hyperactive, and too jittery for school much less a soundstage; and Colette had gotten her scars. That wasn't the end of her connection with *the business*, however. She planned to be a director, "which is better than being a star, because the director has the real power." That there were very few female directors didn't deter her. She said that women who could position themselves to be the tokens to whom men pointed to prove they weren't sexist held a particularly powerful niche in any industry. She was writing a movie that she planned to direct herself, in Europe. When it was finished, she'd make a triumphant return to Hollywood.

Jane spent hours in Colette's bedroom—or, as she came to think of it, her boudoir. Colette slept and lounged and read and wrote on an enormous canopy bed packed with mounds of pillows. An open wardrobe displayed a canny collection of interesting clothes, and necklaces and bracelets dangled from hooks on the walls. Sometimes it was difficult to maneuver a path through the books, laundry, and ashtrays. Colette's mess and preoccupation with feminine totems bespoke an eroticism that Jane admired. It was a far cry from Via's desperate sexuality.

"What if you fall in love?" Jane asked.

Colette was polishing a pair of earrings with dabs of her own spit and the hem of her shirt. "I won't. Not until the time is right, at least."

Jane ran her finger along the beads of a crystal necklace. "Do you really think you can control it? Sometimes it just happens."

"You mean like love at first sight?"

"Like that. Like the way people fall in love."

Colette shrugged. "Don't hold your breath. I'm going to run out of money, and I'll need him to pay me back. I'm sticking this out."

Colette was paying for the house, the parties. She'd won $175,000 in a suit brought by a lawyer she sat next to at a dinner party in Los Angeles who saw potential in the scars he noticed on her hands. He sued the company that made the pajamas she'd been wearing on the night that she stretched her arm across a lit burner on a gas stove and burst into flames. Colette had been thirteen. She took full credit for the advent of flame-retardant sleep clothes for children.

"Have you ever been in love?" Jane pressed.

"How can I have been somewhere that doesn't exist? Love is an illusion. Look at any couple who've been married for a while. Are they in love? No."

Jane tried to think of counterexamples. There were celebrity couples and couples made famous by their correspondence, but she couldn't come up with any she knew firsthand. Nonny and Grand seemed content, but they were hardly in love. Same for Via and Ned Phelps. As for Emlin and Via . . .

Colette saw she'd made her point. "The feeling of being in love is a biological trick to make people have babies. That's it."

"Romantic," Jane said.

"I can live without romance."

"What about sex?"

"What about it?"

"Don't you miss it?"

"I don't miss anything. I have sex. With myself. Sometimes with other people, although it amounts to the same thing."

Jane had never heard a woman admit to masturbation. She smiled, which Colette misunderstood as a critique.

"Jane, do you realize how much freedom I'll have when Nigel inherits? I'm going to be set for life. In the meantime, I've got plenty to do. So do you. You're in no position to fall in love, anyway."

"What do you mean?"

"I mean you're not going to find Prince Charming while you're sitting in your flat scribbling whatever you're scribbling."

Jane was stung. "So what do you suggest I do?"

"I suggest you forget the whole thing."

"No," Jane said. Her forcefulness surprised her. She saw Colette absorb it, and change tacks.

"All right, then. But if you really want to meet someone, you have to go out."

"You mean on dates?"

"It's been done before, Jane."

"Not by me." It was true. In Wynnemoor her friends had moved around in a gang, and only paired off for sex. At college she'd followed the same pattern, augmenting it only with a couple of bouts of unrequited love for men she saw from a distance on whom she could project her fantasies about the perfect mingling of souls. Tall thin men with longish hair who looked like George Harrison. *I'm not too obvious*, she thought.

"All the more reason to get going, I'd say."

Jane had to agree. "Show me the picture," she said suddenly.

"Not this again." Colette gave an exasperated sigh.

"Please."

"I have to remember where I put it."

Jane rolled to her side to watch Colette locate the photo. Colette stood still for a moment and closed her eyes. An expression of confidence appeared on her face and she walked toward what looked like a pile of sweaters. She bent over from her supple waist, her feet turned out from the habit ingrained by childhood ballet lessons, and began to delve. Jane had seen her make the same motions when she kneaded bread.

Suddenly, her hand shot out and she fished a paper from the jetsam. "Okay, here it is." She peered at it for a second, then scowled. "Although I don't know why you like it so much."

Jane reached for it. It was an 8x10 black-and-white photograph taken during Colette's hippie days, when she wore the requisite waist-long hair parted in the middle, a gauzy Mexican blouse closed at the neck by an embroidery thread bow, and a pair of worn hiphuggers. She looked ethereal and perfect.

Jane held it lightly between her fingers and stared.

"What is it about that picture?" Colette was now lifting wet panty hose out of a basin on the floor. She held them up to the light, as if they were negatives.

Jane laid it on her stomach. "It's beautiful. It touches me."

"Why?" Colette was not beyond enjoying a conversation about herself.

"Because I can see who you really are in this picture."

"Oh? And who am I?"

"You're a girl who wants—" Jane broke off, her throat closing. She was thinking *love*.

"Well that's the truth. I am indeed a girl who wants." Whatever she saw in the sheer netting met her standards, for the stockings did not go back in the tub, but were instead rung out and draped over the curtain rod.

"I was ravenous for a cheeseburger when that picture was taken," Colette said.

Jane continued to gaze at it. Perhaps the tender look in Colette's eyes was only a trick of the light. She instructed herself to believe this, not to project onto Colette her own longings. But as she cleared a spot for the picture on the bedside table, she again saw a familiar expression in Colette's eyes. Pining.

. . .

Money was a frequent topic of conversation. Money and makeup.

Colette believed one needed money to be happy. Jane thought the two were separate; her parents had had some money, and it hadn't helped them. Nigel had barely touched money for the first decade and a half of his life and was learning what it was like to consider it at all. In England in 1979 money still had trouble buying class, but it wasn't hard to see how class was inextricably tied to it. Marx had developed his theory of dialectical materialism in England, and living there, Jane began to understand it better. Yet his philosophy had a long way to go against human nature; no one spoke more warmly of queen and crown than the poor.

Colette both supported the egalitarian vision of communism, and thanked God it would never come to pass in her lifetime.

As for makeup, Colette tried to teach Jane how to line her eyes and use a rat-tail comb and a mascara wand. Jane wasn't uncoordinated, but she did feel silly, which made her less intent on steadying her hand. After a couple of sessions, Colette pronounced her ineducable. Jane was relieved to revert to her lip gloss and braid.

Men didn't mind Jane's fresh face. She attracted attention, a phenomenon Colette encouraged her to think of as the equivalent of money; that was, her looks had purchasing power. Jane was never going to adopt that philosophy, but she did begin to be less dismissive when approached. *Less* dismissive; not wide open, like Colette, for whom every wolf whistle led to a full-fledged encounter, even if it amounted to her telling the guy how mistaken he was to have bothered her. Encounters were easy if you didn't care.

Colette convinced Jane of the wisdom of practice. What if she met *the* man and she'd been too stubborn to learn what to say?

In October they were walking in Maida Vale—Jane had read about the canals there—when a red sports car pulled up. Did they want to go to lunch at Peter Sellers's house? Jane automatically shook her head, but Colette folded her arms on his door and began to negotiate. Now? Yes. Can you drive us home so we can change first? No time, Peter's waiting. When will we be back? By six or seven.

"Thanks but no thanks," Colette said in the end.

The well-groomed Englishman displayed his middle finger. "American cunts."

"Oh yeah? Pick on someone your own age."

He patched out. Jane was shaken. Colette took Jane's hand as if she were a child.

"He meant me, not you. You're not a cunt."

"You're not one, either," Jane said.

For once Colette didn't call her to task for her inability to utter certain venerable Anglo-Saxon words, a failing Colette was determined to reverse. Instead she began to walk, leading Jane along. "These so-called canals suck, by the way."

Jane wouldn't have put it like that, but she agreed completely.

.   .   .

There was a man who came to the at homes named Gavin. He worked in a print shop and was in a band, although he'd have listed his credentials the other way around. He lived in a squat in Camden Town with an undulating number of other young people. They stole the electricity for the house from the power lines on the street. Some of the people in his house had come from the neighborhood, and had only gone down to the West End or as far as the Thames once or twice in their lives. Colette had no patience with their attitude;

why the fuck couldn't they get a job at McDonald's? Why couldn't they take a walk and see downtown? But Gavin believed in the subversiveness of unemployment, and understood the limitations that kept them from leaving their own neighborhoods.

"We need the music, you see?" he said.

He was a sylph, thin and pale, with short hair brushed up like Colette's. He dressed the way kids did all over London, in cheap lightweight denim, a leather jacket festooned with pins and safety pins, Doc Martens. He was sweet, and funny, and resolutely anticapitalist. He had a refined mouth, like Candice Bergen, and pain and intelligence in his eyes. His band was called Disband.

"It was either that or Jesus Christ on a Cross," he told Jane.

She laughed. He leaned closer, so their arms touched.

"Come see us play, won't you?"

On Friday night she and Colette arrived at a pub in Islington when the band was already in the middle of the first set. They could hear the music from the street, the driving, high-strung, overamped sound of English punk that made all the sixties music that had been dismissed as noise seem melodic and thoughtfully crafted. Jane had only heard it secondhand, and was curious.

They clomped downstairs to the basement. It was hard to see the room at first, although Gavin was in evidence at the other end of it, dripping sweat, his guitar blocked from sight by the crowd. The core of the audience was bouncing up and down. The sound was spine-rattling.

"Pogoing," Colette said. Yelled.

The cellar stank of beer and cigs. Some of the kids wore swastikas. There was lots of black lipstick to be seen, and raccoon eyes. Colette blended in.

She pushed Jane up to the front, where Gavin spotted her and, forgoing his angry pose for a moment, gave her a nod and a grin. She looked at him, transfixed. What was it about boys playing guitars? She answered herself: emotion. Would he be like that in bed? She wanted Colette's opinion, but it was too loud to talk. They watched for a couple of songs, then Colette pulled her over to the bar.

Jane was thirsty and drank a warm pint quickly, then had to pee. She yelled the word "loo" into Colette's ear, and Colette nodded and got up; she believed women who went out together went to the bathroom together, too. The toilet was back near the steps and the size of a closet, hardly room inside for one, much less the two of them plus the two girls at the mirror who were reapplying their makeup and fiddling with their hair. One had her head shaved to within a tenth of an inch of her skin, with a rickrack pattern carved into it. The other's was green and ratted up.

The one stall was occupied. Jane and Colette crushed against the wall to wait.

"Did you get that done at a shop?" Shaved asked.

Green nodded. "On the King's Road. I like yours."

"Thanks. It's work, though. It grows so fast." She gave a resigned shrug, and then named the upside. "Dad hates it."

"Mine, too."

"You can go to Vidal Sassoon for free," Colette said. "And

you might get picked for a show. Then you get your hair cut in front of hundreds of people."

The girls turned to stare at her; this was valuable information. A girl left the stall and Jane went in. The graffiti touted lesbianism/big cocks. Jane admired the conviction that drove people to take the time to inscribe their predilections. She'd never had sex she felt that strongly about, but knew, intuitively, that such passion existed. She believed the writings on the wall.

She traded places with Colette and reapplied her lip gloss.

"I like *her* hair," Green said.

"It's different, isn't it?" Shaved proclaimed.

They looked at her. Jane touched her braid. "Thank you."

Colette washed her hands and quickly underlined her eyes. The four of them walked out companionably as more black-clothed, white-faced girls barreled in.

The crowd was packed tighter than before, ready for the end of the set. They moved like a piston, and Jane felt obscurely proud of Gavin for being up there, pulling them together. She and Colette tried to get closer to the stage, but it was tough going.

"Fuck it," Colette mouthed. She pointed to the bar, where they could wait this out.

Jane was weaving out of the crowd, seeking its moments of flexibility so she could proceed one body further, then another, when she was suddenly rammed backward. She did not fall down but listed against the people behind as those in front leaned against her. She struggled to straighten up, but her legs pedaled uselessly. There was nothing to do but wait. She couldn't see Colette. The possibility of dying occurred to her, but her mind closed against it. Not here. Not from music. Not yet.

She bent her arms up in front of her chest and breathed deeply and carefully. It wasn't long before she had her footing again. Instead of going to the bar to find Colette, she walked toward the middle of the room to see what had happened. If she saw for herself, she could not imagine worse.

The crowd had pushed back into a circle. There were three kids on the floor, all of them wincing and holding their arms. In the middle of the circle a boy spun around, his arms flung out. Jane saw that he was holding a razor blade. She ran forward and tried to signal Gavin, but the band had lights in their eyes. They played on.

She found Colette, who was also ready to leave. They shoved their way to the door with no pretense of politeness and ran up the steps. They didn't speak until they were far enough from the pub to stop hearing the music. Jane hugged herself. Colette lit a cig.

"Do you think someone called the police?" Jane asked.

"Are you kidding? With all the drugs in there? Anyway, it's a thing here."

"What is?"

"The razor blades. The cutting. It's anarchy."

"It's a luxury, is what it is," Jane said harshly. "For people who don't care about consequences."

Colette looked at her. "I thought you'd be scared."

"I was," Jane said, but she didn't mean she was afraid of a little blood. She was scared of something she'd felt in that room. Desperation.

"The band was scary," Colette said. She sighed. "I guess you're not getting laid tonight."

Gavin didn't appear at the house that weekend. Jane was relieved.

. . .

Jane met an older American man at Jack Straw's Castle who invited her, quite properly, to go out on a date with him another night, and she accepted; he'd asked nicely, after all. She told him where she lived so he could pick her up, but he snapped his fingers and said he was going to be in the West End already, would she mind meeting him? He printed a Mayfair address on the back of a coaster. Nigel recognized it as the address of one of his father's clubs, a men's club, to which women were only welcome in a couple of public rooms. Colette thought Jane was lucky; she'd always wanted to go to one of those places, which she said were very exclusive. Nigel said they were twee, and a bore, which made Jane feel safe.

Colette advised her to splurge on a taxi, but that was Colette. Jane took the tube in her thin floral skirt and green top under a denim jacket and old Pappagallo flats—she couldn't walk in heels. The doorman had her name on a list, and she was guided upstairs to a bar, where Phillip Brown stood waiting. *Seedy*, she thought, but scolded herself for making a snap judgment. Colette's influence. Within minutes, though, he proved her right, as he began to describe porn films that he'd worked on, including a variety Jane had never before known existed, featuring girls with German shepherds and bulls.

"It's a cinch to get the girls," he said. "You have to work to get the animals to play their parts."

Jane tried to give him the benefit of the doubt, but when matters got no better, she developed a headache and left. The next day two cases of champagne were delivered to the vestibule of her building. Why ever had she told him where she lived?

"We'll open these at five o' clock and pour them in the bath," the note read. "I want to bathe you."

Jane pushed the boxes back outside and ran up the hill to Nigel and Colette.

"What did I tell you?" Colette said. "Forget about love. Hang with us."

"Yes, that man is the best my sex has to offer, so forget all of us," Nigel joked.

"I'm not giving up, but I think I'll wait," Jane said, "for the right person."

Colette accepted this new plan with such equanimity that for a moment Jane wondered whose idea the dating had been in the first place. They were both being themselves: Jane doubting her own understanding, and Colette cutting her losses.

"Bathing in champagne. Can you imagine how sticky that would make you?" Colette asked.

"And what's wrong with sticky?" Nigel asked.

. . .

If Colette was willing to allow Jane to wait for the right person to appear, she wasn't prepared to be as permissive about Jane's wardrobe. Among her many talents was shopping, in which she participated at a professional level, albeit unpaid and working only for herself. She didn't go out armed with the pedestrian aim of getting items cheaply; she was looking for the extraordinary; hunting the white leopard. She had a knack for spotting upstairs workrooms where artisans created intermediary stages of an object, such as oddly shaped glass pieces for the tip of a kaleidoscope or ornately carved finials that would eventually don bedposts, and convincing them to sell to her.

"Watch and learn," she said, and Jane was happy to.

One morning, when they were weaving their way down Portobello Road, Jane asked Colette to tell her more about California.

"Everything looks lush, but it's a sham. You lift up a rock in any yard and there's a rattlesnake nest and you have to admit you're in the middle of a desert. A right-wing desert."

"I thought California was liberal."

"No, no, no, no, no. Maman listened to the John Birch radio station every afternoon while she did her exercises. She had no idea he wasn't at the center of American politics." Colette shook her finger. "Remember, Nixon was from Whittier." She clearly felt this one fact made her entire case.

"I wanted to go to Berkeley, but my stepfather refused to pay for it. Berkeley students majored in Marxism or macramé. Neither course was worthy of his inherited money."

"He did you a favor," Colette said.

"Did he? Perhaps." She considered it. "If I'd gone out there at eighteen, I probably wouldn't have come here now."

"*Exactement.* There's a reason for everything."

"A silver lining?"

"Let's make it a silver bracelet. Better yet, a necklace."

Jane tried it out. "Every disappointment has a silver necklace." She smiled.

Colette stopped to examine a tray of jewelry. "Nothing," she pronounced, and moved them on.

They passed a shop called Winthrop's.

"All the names here are so familiar," Jane said. "I went to school with Eleanor Winthrop. I know Hancocks and Smiths and Robertses and Morrises. I suppose they're all related, from hundreds of years ago."

Colette peered at a window full of leather jackets. "Who needs it?"

Jane sighed. "Where I grew up, people were always trying to place you and figure out exactly which branch of which family you were from and when you arrived in the New World. My father's family came early, but they weren't from Philadelphia, and my mother's family who were had no money. I always felt inadequate."

"You resented it."

"I wish I had. That would have been healthier, I think. Instead, I wanted the impossible—to be the girl with the rich handsome father who spoils her and the family heirlooms scattered carelessly around the house. When we went on class trips to the Liberty Bell, my friends pointed out where their great, great-etcetera-grandfathers had signed the Declaration of Independence. I envied that." She looked at Colette. "I wanted to be burdened with traditions and obligations. I wanted to be able to walk into school and roll my eyes and say I couldn't go to such and such a party because *we* always had our family reunion on this particular weekend every year."

"All I ever wanted was to meet someone who'd read a book." Colette fished a cig out of her bag with long purple fingernails.

"What about your mother's family?"

"They have that French snobbery, but it's cultural more than lineal. In France you can be a peasant and still look down your nose at a duke if he doesn't know his wines."

"You know your wines."

Colette peeled a fleck of tobacco from her tongue. "So what? There are other things in life. Your talent and ambition. Do you think your old D.A.R. friends are working on their poetry?"

"They weren't in the D.A.R. It's *arriviste*. The Colonial Dames is the ticket."

A beautiful coffee-colored man in flowing baggy pants and even more flowing dreadlocks walked by. Colette nodded at him coolly as he passed and he nodded back. The international language of appreciation. Jane was too discreet to look at him directly, but when he was out of hearing distance, she made her approval known. "Wow. He could change my mind about meaningless encounters."

Colette rolled her eyes. "I think," she said as she linked an arm through Jane's, "you should begin to believe you have better things to do. Don't you want to be famous?"

"Famous?"

"Yes, famous. As in people you'll never meet know who you are, and you get invited to A-list parties. I'm going to have Los Angeles kissing my feet when my movie comes out. Nigel's writing the great English novel. What about you?"

"I never thought about it." It was true. Fame was for other people.

"Jane, Jane, Jane. What am I going to do with you?" Before Jane could answer, Colette thrust out her arm. "Wait a minute." They'd come abreast of a row of old wooden barrels. "White shirts," Colette said, rifling. "I want you to buy a few. You can never have too many."

Jane reached into a barrel and swished her hand among the old, pure materials until she felt something so smooth and soft and sensuous that it gave her a chill. She pulled it up and saw she'd unearthed a wedding dress. She held it up to herself, clasping the bodice under her chin and pulling the skirt around her hips. The satin was mottled with age stains, but nevertheless alluring and heavy, which seemed symbolically appropriate. It occurred to her that it was the first time she'd ever been as close to such a dress. Via and Nonny had chosen to be married in suits, so there'd been no carefully wrapped and preserved gowns in the family attics, and at friends' weddings she'd always been at arm's length—looking but not touching.

"How about this?" she called out.

"Just a sec." Colette flipped through a rack of dresses. Jane smiled at her shopping outfit of heavy DM's, a jean jacket festooned with incongruously ladylike pins, her spiky hair brushed straight up and dotted here and there with small bow-shaped barrettes. It was a far cry from the tweed suits Nonny wore when she took Jane to Best & Co. Eventually, Colette looked her way and, immediately upon seeing the dress, strode over.

She gathered a pinch of the material between her discerning fingers, testing it. "Good quality," she pronounced. "I wonder what it was doing in there?"

"It looks like a museum piece," Jane whispered. She couldn't bring herself to bargain, but she was open to a good find.

The proprietor of the stall appeared—they always spotted Jane as someone who could be talked into buying. He was a thin middle-aged man with large dark eyes and a dark blue-gray skin who she guessed was from Turkey or India. Perhaps that explained why he hadn't recognized the dress for what it was and had plonked it in with the blouses.

"Want to try?" he asked, holding his arm solicitously at right angles to his body like a maître d'. She couldn't imagine where he wanted her to change. The stall was outside, in the middle of a parking lot. But in a far corner, against a wall, he'd fashioned a dressing room out of Indian bedspreads hung on a clothesline. It brought to mind stories about the white slave trade and girls snatched from dressing rooms in boutiques. But that was in Paris.

"Yes, she does."

"I do?"

"You do. Come on."

Colette had gathered a pile of dresses herself. Beautiful, ephemeral dresses, made of materials that were no longer readily available. Again she'd proven her talent in the bazaar. Jane touched the cloth of a blue dress. It felt like a butterfly wing.

"Okay," Colette said, "put it on."

"No thanks. You try it if you like it so much."

"I want to see how it looks. I'm in the market for a wedding dress, remember."

"Have you set a date?"

"Nigel has to talk to his parents. He wants to do it in person, but he doesn't want to go down there. If he doesn't do it soon, I'm going to take matters into my own hands." She held the dress up. "Please?"

Jane was disarmed by Colette's rare attitude of vulnerability. "Okay. But you owe me."

Jane lifted it high, put her hands into the arms, and then let go. The dress fell heavily, the stiff bodice grazing her breasts. She arranged it as well as she could over her tee shirt and jeans. She reached back for a zipper, but instead her fingers found a placket with dozens of satin buttons opposite dozens of delicate satin loops. Jane could never notice such details without picturing ten-year-old girls sewing frantically in a dark room, praying their fingers wouldn't bleed onto the material. She sighed, thinking she had too active a conscience to ever be really rich—which was too bad, because she'd like the stays in really good hotels, and the wherewithal to buy extravagant Christmas presents.

"Don't bother with the buttons," she said over her shoulder to Colette. "I'm not going to keep it on for very long."

"As if I was even considering doing them. You need a special hook for that, anyway."

Jane went to the mirror, a five-foot leaning rectangle. It was impossible to gauge the effect accurately. There was just a cloud of white, and then her head. The angle of the glass made her middle look thick, like a shotgun bride.

"I don't feel like myself."

"You're not supposed to. A wedding is a pageant and the bride has a role to play. It's for the community more than the couple."

"What about the mystical union? You don't think people feel that, when they are pronounced man and wife?"

Colette wagged her finger. "No, no, no, no, no. It's about dowry and blood lines and power and patriarchy. The whole point of marriage is so that men know who their children are. They'd never be able to tell if women were screwing everybody. It's a control thing, that's all." She pulled at the skirts, fluffing them out. "There's no way to get rid of stains like that. Luckily, Nigel doesn't want a big wedding anyway. He wants to get married in a registry office. Just as well. These dresses make everyone look like an opera singer."

"So why did you want me to try it on?" Jane shrugged her shoulders out of the sleeves. Colette helped her remove it and flung it over the length of clothesline that served as hooks and hangers.

"To confirm my opinion. I hope this one fits," Colette said, picking up the butterfly dress. "Go look for blouses while I try these. You need two, at least."

Jane reached for the wedding dress.

"Leave it. I'll bring everything out together."

Jane ducked under the bedspread-curtain. She was half-way back to the barrels when she realized her shoulder felt strange; she was missing the weight of her bag. She returned to the dressing room and slipped back through the opening.

"Did I leave my bag in here?" she asked, and then she saw Colette.

There was normal skin here and there, but most of her body was covered with bands of opalescent skin that looked like the insides of clam shells, smooth and shiny. At the edges of those furrows was darker crinkled flesh that made Jane wince. Although Colette didn't turn around, Jane knew that the scarring was as extensive on her front.

"Colette—"

"Leave," Colette said, without turning around.

Jane hesitated for a moment, wanting to say something more.

"I know, I know," Colette said wearily. "Thank you. It's okay. There—we've had the conversation. Now. Please. Go."

Jane obeyed, her stomach knitting. It wasn't that she was bothered by the scars. What she couldn't stand was the thought of Colette being hurt.

It was a long time before Colette emerged from the tent. While she waited, Jane picked carefully through the blouses, examining them for stains and fraying hems. When Colette appeared, Jane ran to show her the three she'd chosen.

"They're mint condition, aren't they?" she said. If there was nothing else she could do to comfort Colette, she could at least demonstrate that she'd learned something from her.

Colette glanced at them. "They'll do."

"Colette—"

"I don't want to talk about it."

Jane flinched but stood her ground. "When you do, you can talk to me."

Colette reached her arm out and around Jane's neck, then stepped into an embrace. "Thank you," she said next to Jane's ear.

In the next instant, she was all authority again as she handed the proprietor several dresses and began to dicker with him over the price. To Jane's surprise, she bought the wedding dress. She gave an explanation when she saw Jane's wide eyes.

"It might be fun to have for a costume party. Or as they say here, fancy dress."

. . .

Via wrote with a bi-weekly regularity that Jane soon came to count on, in the way that people living far from home tend to make much of the mail. Her letters were short, focusing mainly on descriptions of nature. She wasn't moved to impart much family news, which Jane supposed was because as a family they'd experienced such a cataclysm that Alex's soccer goal or Caroline's college applications didn't qualify as anything but ephemera and weren't worth writing down. Jane wondered about this new mother she found in the letters. She took them to Colette for a diagnosis. Colette claimed to practice all the magic arts, including handwriting analysis.

"Hmm. I'm not really crazy about these loops." Colette pointed to the offending squiggles with a newly green nail. "And look at the way her capitals slant. I'd say she's a narcissist, and timid, too. That's a bad combination. People like that can be real bullies on their own turf." She laid the tissues of air-mail paper down. "You had it rough," she said definitively, as if she'd just seen a documentary on the subject.

"Colette, did you read the letters?" The page on top was a lovely description of purpling leaves. Via missed the scent of smoking leaf piles; burning had been banned.

"I don't need the content when I have the subtext."

Jane folded the letters and put them back in her knapsack. She liked Colette coming to her defense, but she liked receiving the letters, too. "If you *had* read them," she said, "you'd know my Uncle Francis is coming to town. He's taking me out to dinner."

"Somewhere good?"

The quality of the restaurant hadn't crossed Jane's mind. She'd barely seen Francis in years, except at weddings and other family events, of which there hadn't been many.

"I suppose so. He likes the finer things."

"Can we come?"

"Come where?" Nigel entered the kitchen, his hair

mussed and his tie blown over his shoulder. Jane thought she heard Colette suck in her breath, but when she looked over, Colette appeared perfectly serene. She explained about the dinner.

"I think we should go, don't you?" Colette said.

"Perhaps Jane wants to see him alone. Anyway, I have class that night. My teacher doesn't look kindly on absences."

"I want to go," Colette said.

"Maybe it would be better to wait for next time," Jane said gently.

As always, Colette made a swift recovery. "We have to start planning Thanksgiving." She went over to the cupboards and began to rummage. "I know I have some allspice in here somewhere."

Nigel and Jane exchanged glances. A project was getting underway, and they knew what that meant. "I'm going up," Nigel said. He grabbed a box of biscuits off the counter. "See you later!"

Colette found several delicacies of interest and pulled them all down. "He's been working hard. I really think he's talented."

"How's your movie going?"

"Oh, you know."

Jane didn't know, but it appeared she wasn't about to find out. Colette began counting glasses. "I'm going to have to buy a few things."

Jane heard sounds from upstairs, as if furniture were being moved around, and wondered what they had to do with writing a book. Colette didn't seem to notice.

"Write this down, will you?" she said, and began to dictate a to-do list.

. . .

Francis had made reservations at a restaurant in Knightsbridge, far out of Jane's usual orbit. When she arrived, with both formality and irony, he lifted her hand to his lips and properly kissed the air above it. Jane felt a prick of regret about not bringing Colette as she took in Francis's perfectly cut suit and starched, pristine cuffs; Colette would appreciate his efforts. Like many handsome men, his looks had kept improving as he matured, so that nearing fifty he was a head turner whereas earlier he'd been merely notable. His former bulkiness had slipped away, leaving him sleek and refined. He groomed himself carefully. Yet the total effect he created, because of the discernible earnest calculations and hours dedicated to that end, was one of exuberant innocence, even in middle age. He tried to pass himself off as a sybarite, but he retained too much the aura of the schoolboy for that to be convincing. She thought he was beginning to look a lot like Nonny, but considering the strained relationship he and Via had always had with their parents, she decided to keep the observation to herself.

They were led to a table near the front window. "My stock has risen," Francis said. "The last time I was here, I was put by the kitchen. It must be you."

"Or the bill you pressed into his palm." Jane laid her napkin on her lap. She could be droll when she wanted to. England had made her want to.

"Okay. Or that. But you look lovely, either way."

She almost told him that she was being tutored in beauty, but she stopped herself, on the grounds of feminine mystique.

His eyes scanned the room restlessly. "There's Viscount Linley. And there's Diana Spencer, who's rumored to be seeing Prince Charles . . ." He named names. Jane knew only the most famous. He sighed.

"I haven't done a good job with you. When you were little, I planned to take you under my wing. But then when you moved in with . . ." He hesitated.

"Your parents?" Her tone contained a light tease. While she was growing up, it had been difficult for her to understand his estrangement from Nonny and Grand, who'd provided her with whatever sense of stability she'd had after Emlin's death; she and the other children had lived with them until Via remarried. Now, in light of the distance between her and Via, it didn't seem so incomprehensible. Her teasing was empathetic, and he could tell.

"Exactly. First them, and then the even less *simpatico* Ned Phelps. I gave up. I apologize for that."

She was surprised. "It wasn't your fault."

He didn't respond immediately. He became thoughtful and sat back and crossed his legs. "One of the hardest things, I think, is to know when one stops being the child and starts being the adult. Via and I remained children for way too long."

Jane had never considered this. In her eyes, Via was too powerful not to be an adult.

"Should I not talk about this?" Francis asked.

"No. I want to hear."

"I stopped coming to see you because I didn't want to see the people around you. That was childish of me. You were the real child. I was too wrapped up in my own misery to give you your due."

He meant Via. He was apologizing for her, too.

"What I'm saying might be difficult for you to understand," he went on, "because you stopped being a child a long time ago."

Her eyes filled. He slid his hand across the table toward her, and she laid her fingers in his. "I hope to get to know you now, if you'll let me," he said.

She didn't hesitate. Hadn't she gotten away from the past, including its regrets and recriminations? Three thousand miles and an ocean away. She leaned across the table and kissed his smooth, spice-scented cheek.

"Thank you," he said.

"What would you have taught me?" she asked when she sat back down.

"To marry well. You were to be my stand-in in the world of matrimony. I'd have liked to marry a prince, but clearly I couldn't. So you were going to fulfill that dream for me."

"Sorry I missed out on that training."

"I don't suppose I could start molding you now?"

"I'm afraid it's too late. I'm holding out for true love. And a career, by the way."

"Oh dear. You sound like me."

"Thanks, I think."

"The career is easy enough, but the true love? Is there any way I could talk you out of it?"

"It doesn't sound as though you talked yourself out of it."

"I'm just trying to spare you some heartache. But I've lived long enough to know that we all have to learn our own lessons. What are you drinking?"

"I'm learning beer."

He winced.

"Sherry?"

"Better."

Francis waved his fingers, and within seconds a waiter appeared with the drink. Jane felt a flush of confidence as she took the delicate glass from the tray.

"So. I thought dancing after dinner. Does that suit?" Francis took his cigarette case from his jacket. She got a jolt from seeing it; it was the same one he'd had when she was a child. She remembered he'd offered her a cig on the night her father died.

"As long as it's not in the basement of a pub."

"This will be fun, I promise."

They smiled shyly at the same time and laughed at their awkwardness. It was odd to feel so familiar without really knowing each other.

Francis raised his glass. "Chin-chin," Francis said. "Or as I like to think of it, double chin."

Jane clinked with him. "You don't have one. You look very fit."

"Have to. No one wants a slug handling their art."

"How is business, anyway?"

Francis had come to buy some treasures for the museum. A duke was quietly selling off the family pictures so he could afford to hold onto the family land, a scenario Francis described with a combination of regret for the harsh realities of modern life and amusement at the loftiness of the dilemma. Francis would assess the authenticity of the paintings and set the parameters for a price. The duke didn't want them to go to auction.

"Not because he's ashamed of his penury," Francis said. "It's aristocratic to be land-rich, cash-poor. He just doesn't want some Arab taking his Holbein to Beverly Hills."

"I guess if an English aristocrat can't be a snob, who can?"

"I can. Someone has to maintain the standards, after all. It might as well be me."

Jane smiled and raised her glass this time. "To your snobbish standards. Yours and Colette's."

Francis followed suit. "I never refuse a toast, even if I don't know who it's to." He sipped and then offered her a Marlboro.

"Colette is my friend, and she would love these. She says they taste completely different here." She waved the case away.

"Still pure, eh? I'm so sorry. I could have corrupted you so stylishly. Is it too late?"

"For cigarettes, yes."

He sighed. "All right. So Colette. Does she smoke a lot?"

"She's a chimney."

"Then you have my approval for the friendship. I'll give you the rest of my carton for her."

"She wanted to come tonight. She invited herself, as we used to say at Miss Dictor's."

"I *do* like her! But I'm glad to have you alone. Now tell me about you. How did you get from there to here? I must say, I'm impressed and intrigued."

Normally, she'd have provided a brief answer to his question. Fine. Great. So-so. She'd developed that habit early on, having taken to heart what Nonny said about most people wanting to hear only a quick and positive response to any question. Brevity was an armor, and she was inclined to protect herself. Yet the hold of that old habit seemed to have lost its power. It may have been because of Francis, who could be counted on to behave as though he'd seen it all. It may have been a chance to show what she was learning from Colette without the teacher being there to watch and possibly make her nervous. It may have been her own determination to change, her readiness to take risks, or even the night, the luxury of the heavy silver and dim lighting, the sense of being at the center of the English-speaking world, where language was a secular god. For whatever reason, she declined to offer the perfunctory monosyllabic response, and instead told him the truth about why she'd left and what had happened to her since. She knew she sounded young and earnest and was no doubt describing a path worn by many other girls before her, yet she wasn't bothered by being unoriginal. She was speaking of matters original to her, and when she began to describe Nigel and Colette, she was certain of being on fresh ground. To her gratification, he was particularly interested in their story, and it was all she could do to keep from falling under the spell of his interest to the point of pandering. She drew a firm line at mentioning Colette's scars, but she didn't see any harm in portraying Nigel's attractions. She was proud of her friends.

"He reminds me of Sebastian Flyte," she said. Francis had been the one to give her a copy of *Brideshead Revisited* for her sixteenth birthday.

"I'm envious. I always wanted to be Sebastian—wildly popular at Oxford, and dead at an early age from some tawdry disease like alcoholism or gonorrhea. Then my parents would be sorry!"

"They would," Jane agreed. She pictured Nonny and Grand standing together in their driveway, waving goodbye to her. "I wanted to be Julia, but I knew I was Cordelia."

"True. If there'd been a war in Wynnemoor, you'd have been the one to turn Ned Phelps's house into a hospital."

"I'm not like that anymore."

"It doesn't bother me if you are. Someone has to be responsible."

"Yes, but not me. Not this year."

"I'm glad to hear it. You were too responsible as a child. Too strict. A little headmistress."

"There's a nice image."

"Via and I had to hide from you. You noticed everything."

"I didn't want to be that way. I just was."

He gave her a kind smile. "As your godfather, I give you permission to be oblivious."

"Thank you, Uncle Francis. I'll try."

. . .

They went to a club called Heaven, where she was one of the only women in a crowd of dozens, maybe hundreds of men. She might have felt uncomfortable there if it weren't for Francis and his gentlemanly manners. He stayed at her side all night—except when she excused him to dance with men who signaled him so subtly that most of the time she couldn't even see the beckoning. The hours disappeared; the sky was already streaked when they came out again. There were no cabs to be seen, but Francis went to a phone and called a service and soon they were in a cozy back seat, speeding home. She was exhausted but alert.

"I'm glad to see you so happy," he said. "Your mother would be, too."

Jane wasn't sure about that. Would Via even notice? "I'm glad to see *you*, Uncle Francis. I was a little afraid of it, but it was really fun."

"You don't have to be afraid of me." He took her hand. "I was afraid of you, too, actually."

"Me?"

"That you blamed me. For that night."

She knew which night he meant. "I think Via blames me," she said.

"I've thought about it a million times, but I don't know what I could have done."

A thought occurred to her. "Francis—was it you who took the phone off the hook?"

"No. No, I didn't."

"Via said it was me, but I don't remember."

He reached out his bear's arm—a lean bear now—and pulled her next to him. "That wasn't it, you know. Even if you did do it, what happened wasn't your fault."

Jane leaned her head on his shoulder. She wished she believed him. They rode silently until the car stopped in front of her house.

"Well," Francis said. "I should get back to the hotel and see if my duke has called with second thoughts. They usually do. It's part of the game."

"You're leaving tonight?"

He nodded.

"You wouldn't like to meet my friends this afternoon, would you? They have their at home starting at four."

"Is this the Sebastian character?"

"Yes."

"You really don't mind sharing your life with an old fart like me?"

"Old fart" was one of Grand's expressions.

"I'd like it very much."

. . .

Nigel was walking circles in the back garden. Jane had run so fast up the hill that she'd barely noticed the weather, but she saw now what a beautiful day it was. Particles of—what? the afternoon?—hung suspended in sun shafts. Leaves broke

119

from branches with a tiny jerk, and floated on quirky pathways to the ground. The air was balmy. She wondered why everyone wasn't outside.

"Hi, Nigel. I'm looking for my Uncle Francis. Did he come here? I told him to. Then I overslept."

She'd startled him. He snapped his head up and slipped his hands in his pockets. For an instant he looked at her without recognition.

"I'm sorry, I'm disturbing you. I'll talk to you later." She turned to go back inside.

"No, no—wait, Jane." He reached out his hand toward her. "I was, as they say, lost in thought."

He gave her one of his smiles, which now contained affection as well as charm, and she walked back toward him. "I hope I didn't interrupt genius," she said lightly.

He shook his head. "I can't claim that. Not now, not ever."

"Don't let Colette hear you deprecate yourself that way. No, no, no, no, no," she said, wagging her finger, mimicking Colette's French way of scolding.

He made a mock shudder. "Thank you for reminding me. Thou shalt be self-confident is one of the top commandments around here. That, and thou shalt not be a bore."

"How about thou shalt not wear polyester."

"Thou shalt not be ordinary."

"Thou shalt not have a quiet evening at home alone."

"Thou shalt not sweat."

"Thou shalt not fall in love."

Nigel broke into a broad smile and jangled the change in

his pockets. "We could play this game all day. So many rules, so few rewards."

He was still smiling. Making conversation, she decided.

"I was just looking for my Uncle Francis. Perhaps he didn't come after all."

"Oh yes he did. He was here, all right."

She couldn't quite discern the sense of his tone. "Did anything happen?"

"Happen?"

"Was he all right? We were out all night and then he had to go right to work . . ."

"He was fine, Jane. Kind of great, actually." He pointed his toe out in front of him as if he were dipping it in a pond. "He said he's coming back in a couple of months." He looked at her for affirmation, and she smiled accommodatingly, although Francis hadn't mentioned another trip. "He said maybe he could help me find a job of some sort. It's time I do something."

It hadn't occurred to her that he did nothing. She'd adopted Colette's faith in his book.

"What kind of job?"

"I don't know. I'm willing to try anything. At this point I'd just like to make my own money. I have to think ahead. Colette's so sure everything is going to go according to her plan, but what if she's wrong? In any case, I need a career. I want to do work, real work."

"I'm sure you could do anything you want," Jane said. She realized she hadn't talked to him alone for a while, except for jokes.

He raised his eyebrows. "Really? My experience has been just the opposite."

He turned away and walked off toward the back of the garden. She stayed where he'd left her, wondering if she should go after him or let him alone. It was so hard to know what was right.

"Jane! Up here!"

She visored her eyes and spotted Colette waving from the dining room window. "Come on up! Where have you been?"

"Coming!" she called.

She turned to wave at Nigel, but he was looking upwards at a low-flying plane.

ON THANKSGIVING DAY, AFTER preparing four pans of corn pudding from Nonny's secret recipe, Jane sat at the small table in her flat, fully intending to work. She was writing a poem about Cape May, where Nonny and Grand had their summer house. The day before, it had seemed promising, but now she couldn't think, at least not about black-eyed Susans and Baltimore orioles. Hard as she tried to be diligent, her thoughts lapsed away from word choice and line breaks to the more pertinent question—or impertinent—of what she should wear. It was a question she'd begun to explore with growing regularity, and for which Colette was to blame. Think of yourself as a poem, Colette had roared in an exasperated moment, and Jane had finally gotten it. She was still a novice, however. Her feel for the subjects of couture and maquillage was in the early stages of development, and she dared not go very far on her own. They weren't subjects that came naturally; she'd never been able to answer the rudimentary question posed by fashion magazines about the shape of her face. "It's round," Colette told her at a glance. "Mine's heart-shaped. See?" But Jane couldn't, not even after having had the matter so decisively settled.

When after an hour she hadn't come up with a single new line, she decided it was no use, and she began instead to rifle her tiny closet. It took some doing—she longed for the familiarity of her jeans—but eventually she decided on a long brown velvet skirt, an old pale pink cashmere sweater inherited from Via's college days, and knee-high brown boots. The three gold bracelets that Ned Phelps had given her for her sixteenth birthday. Gold hoop earrings. Lipstick, green eye shadow, and a touch of blush on her cheekbones. She tried pinning her hair up, but she felt too naked without it on her neck, so she wore her usual braid. At some point during her preparations, she realized she wanted to look attractive. She was twenty-three years old, and she'd never allowed herself to think much about her looks or the impression she was making; or, more accurately, she'd never been allowed. Now, in spite of Via's dictums against shallowness and superficiality, Jane was ready to take the risk. When she'd finished dressing, she looked in the mirror and thought she looked like herself, polished. She decided to never again be persuaded that there was anything wrong with that.

Nigel had arranged for someone to give her a ride to the party, to help her carry the food, and at a quarter to three she pulled the heavy pans from the oven and set them on the table to cool. Just as she began to sponge the counter—all except her leftover plate from lunch that she was leaving out for the mouse—a line came to her, *the monks walk back from their swim / in the eye of the wind.* She repeated it to herself as she located pencil and paper, and scribbled an entire poem down in a transcendent few minutes. When she'd finished, it took her a moment to regain her bearings; it was as if she'd been somewhere else entirely, in a deep dream or a parallel universe. She couldn't wait to describe it to Colette, who'd surely know exactly what she meant—was there any experience about which Colette wasn't an expert? She was about to reread the poem when footsteps thudded up the stairs. She glanced around the room. Her coat was on the back of the chair. The mouse was nowhere in sight. Her bed looked neat and, even with its bright Indian bedspread, more like a monastic palette than an erotic venue. Next to the pudding pans, her typewriter and stack of pages were squared off and symmetrical. Back of them sat her dictionary and thesaurus, both paperback. She kept her pens and pencils in a jar on the windowsill. She'd decorated in the spirit of minimalism, for serenity and lack of distraction. Her flat was exactly the way she wanted it, so she hadn't been offended when Colette said it looked like the prep school dorm room of a very serious Taiwanese foreign exchange student. Instead the accuracy of the description made her laugh.

The footsteps stopped on the landing. She took a silent step closer to the door. It occurred to her that she had no idea who was coming for her. Had Colette ever told her who it would be? She didn't think so. It shocked her that she'd become so loose that she hadn't even asked. She should have asked. She had an impulse to change her clothes, but it was too late for that. *No failures of nerve*, she reminded herself. She turned the handle.

ALICE ELLIOTT DARK

"Hello?" To her surprise, she found herself looking not at a person, but at a person's chest. Awkwardly, she looked up. "Are you my ride?"

He shrugged. "I don't have a car."

Jane took a step backward and prepared to shut the door again. "I'm sorry. I was expecting someone. To take me to a party," she added. She was flustered. Why was he there? The only other flat on the floor belonged to a banker, and she always worked late. Jane had never known her neighbor to have any visitors, much less a large, handsome American.

He didn't go away. Instead he leaned forward and squinted at the name card she'd taped to the door when she'd first moved in.

"Jane MacLeod?"

She nodded.

"Friend of Nigel Kirby-Kerr?"

"Yes."

He straightened up. "It looks like I'm your man. The ride part, however, is going to be a problem."

He's too old for me, she thought. The point being that she was thinking about it. At first sight.

He tapped at his watch. "The party's only going to last eight hours or so."

"Sorry. Come in."

He was too tall to walk directly through the door; he'd have to stoop, and she stepped back to give him room to make the maneuver. She had an impulse to apologize for his inconvenience, but that would draw undue attention to the anomaly of his height. It seemed wrong, though, not to say

126

something, to just stand by and watch, anxiously, sideways, the lintel where his head might hit, pretending she didn't notice. "Careful," she murmured. He raised his eyes to see her even as he ducked down. He kept his eyes on her as he straightened up. He was nearly as tall as the ceiling, and thin. She saw shoulder-length thick dark hair, discernible bones in a good face, a straight nose, a mustache, and a look of humor and intelligence. She couldn't tell for sure about his eyes; they were too deep-set to reveal a color in the dim hall light.

"Thank you," he said, "for your concern." He bounced his elbows against his sides. His hands were in his pockets and his jacket flapped like wings. It was a fringed buckskin jacket, like a cowboy.

"You're welcome. As the sign says, I'm Jane MacLeod." She put out a hand, but he didn't respond in kind. Quickly, she wrapped her arms around her waist, as if this were the gesture she'd been making.

"Clay West."

She nodded, hugging herself harder. Why had he said *I'm your man?*

"So I'm supposed to help you carry something?" He looked around. She had no sense of what he was thinking. Not of her, she told herself quickly.

"I made corn pudding. It's my grandmother's recipe. Corn, butter, and sugar."

"Sounds horrible." He shuddered.

"What do you mean? Butter and sugar are surefire." Surefire? Had she ever used that expression before?

"Then I guess it's the corn that disturbs me."

She laughed, sharply, surprising them both. He cocked his head. His hair grazed his shoulders. He gave a small, appraising nod. She crossed her arms.

"How do you know Nigel and Colette?" she asked.

"I only know Nigel. He's in my class."

"You're learning to write, too?"

"Hm. Am I learning to write, am I learning to write?"

Instead of answering, he turned away from her and looked at the room. He took his time; she saw his gaze flicking from belonging to belonging. It disconcerted her until she figured it out; he was doing a writing exercise. Sizing her up by means of her possessions. *I told you to decorate*, she heard Colette say.

He faced her again. His eyes were blue. "I'm Nigel's teacher."

"Oh. I'm sorry." Her lips caught on her teeth. He unsettled her.

"You didn't know. And, anyway, yes, I'm learning to write. Each piece finds its own form. I'm also becoming certain that you can only learn to write by writing. A teacher can't do much for you, except terrify you into meeting deadlines. Did Dickens have a teacher? Or Flaubert?"

He'd stepped closer to her, and emphasized each name by poking toward her with his long index finger. No wonder Nigel had been afraid to miss class.

"Actually, I don't know," he said. "I doubt it, though. The point is, no one needs a writing teacher."

"Why do you teach, if you think that?"

"Money. So I can keep writing."

"It's honest of you to admit it."

"I have no secrets. If you want to protect yourself, practice full disclosure."

"That sounds like a good theme for a story."

"I thought so. I wrote it. It was called 'A Clear, Clean Man.' It was in *The O. Henry Prize Stories of 1976*. It got me the job at Antioch."

He spoke as if she knew about the job at Antioch, and she placed him as one of those people who talk in an all-encompassing shorthand, assuming the world was up to speed. Her brother Alex spoke like that, including in his conversations the first names of people she'd never heard of, as if they were all old buds. She'd always been both bemused and envious of the posture. What would it be like to present yourself with such aplomb, counting on people to absorb your life like breath—or to not care if they didn't?

As she thought about it, Clay West stacked all four heavy pans on top of each other and picked them up.

"Let me." She reached to take the top one.

He shrugged as if it didn't matter to him either way how many he carried. Or if she helped. Or that she was trying to be polite. She lifted two off, then realized she needed her coat and put them back down again.

"Congratulations," she said, about his story. "That's quite an accomplishment. It must have been really exciting when they picked it."

"I was glad for the sake of my *career*, but it has nothing to do with me. Or the story. It was the same story when it was in a journal. The imprimatur didn't improve it."

As he spoke, she held the hems of her sleeves in her palms and threaded her arms into her pea coat. He didn't offer to help her, but he was watching.

"I'm sure it reached a lot more people, though, in *O. Henry*. That must have been gratifying."

He shifted gears adroitly. "The more the merrier!"

She didn't want to let him get away with the maneuver. "Is that how you do it?"

"What?"

"Implement your policy of full disclosure? By saying what you feel, but making it a joke?"

He stared at her. She didn't blame him. She didn't know what was clever and what was going too far. Colette was right about needing practice.

"You don't have to help me if you don't want to. You can go."

"No, no." He picked up the pans. "I'm your man."

His hair slipped over his forehead and a warm flush went through her. Why did he keep saying that? They stepped into the hall. She turned the key in the lock and then suddenly was anxious.

"Oh," she said. "Wait a minute. I think I may have forgotten something."

She hurried back to her tiny kitchen. The stove had been turned off, as had the taps in the sink. Everything looked as tidy and impersonal as it had the day she moved in, when the landlord had handed her a key and a bucket of cleaning products. She returned to the hall and locked up quickly.

"Everything's fine. I'll take two of those." She lifted them off his pile. He didn't argue about it.

"After you," he said.

She walked through the downstairs door with her head bent low, squinting to protect her eyes from the cold, wishing she had her hands free to turn her collar up, but it was warmer outside than she'd imagined. She'd expected to walk out into the weather of a Thanksgiving Day at home; a gray wet chill, pale yellow sky, the grass shriveled and crunchy underfoot; but the temperature was mild, with a balmy breeze. She shifted the pans to her right hip and began to step gingerly down the five risers to the sidewalk. Don't fall, she told herself. She cringed as the door dropped shut behind her. Behind him. She wished, now, that she'd insisted he go first, so she'd be the one following—and watching. On the bottom step she reached her leg out further and was caught up short by the tight skirt, which threw her off balance for a moment. She stepped down to the pavement and he drew up beside her. Her pea coat was too warm; beads of perspiration trickled down her back, catching at her waistband.

"So," he said.

A car whizzed by and blew the leaves in the street back toward the curb. Behind her she heard the sash of a window rattle.

"So I guess we should walk to the tube," she said.

"Or we could walk all the way," he said. "Let's walk. I'll carry the pans when you get tired."

"All right."

"I walk all over London." He looked at her over his shoulder as he moved ahead of her. "They try to claim some of the buildings here are hundreds of years old. I don't believe it. In California they rip houses down after twenty years."

"You'd really hate Rome," Jane teased.

"Don't I know it. No way I'm going there."

Jane dipped her chin to hide her amusement as she stepped carefully off the curb into the street. *Don't fall, don't fall*, she told herself. By the time they were halfway to Hampstead, she realized the phrase was a metaphor. She managed to keep her footing, but otherwise the warning didn't steady her. She had to walk purposefully to keep from drifting his way.

. . .

Every chair and sofa held people eating with plates on their laps. Jane sat with a group who were discussing the monarchy. It was the same style of conversation she'd heard all her life—moot disapproval—and she remained detached until the subject of Charles's future came up.

"I saw Diana Spencer in a restaurant," she offered, but it wasn't, apparently, a serious enough addition to the talk. People looked at her for a second, then looked away.

"She's very pretty," she added stubbornly.

She glanced across the room to where Clay was standing among a group of admirers: the writing class, she assumed. He smiled broadly and was very animated. In spite of knowing she had no right to, she felt proud of his popularity. She hadn't spoken to him since they'd arrived, but she knew where he was. Every minute.

When she finished her food, she took her plate to the kitchen. Colette walked by and squeezed her arm.

"How are you doing? More important, how's my mascara? I can't even get to the bathroom to check. I hate turkey. Can you believe this crowd?"

"It's a great party," Jane said. "I want to talk to you." She suddenly felt a child's need to tell, to make it real.

"Later. Stay after. Dish and dish."

Jane was about to say no, talk to me now, when someone came up and asked Colette for a Band-Aid. They all looked down at his dripping thumb. "Swiss Army–knife accident," he explained.

"Those things should be banned," Colette said, leading him off. As they retreated, Jane heard Colette telling him that the Swiss weren't nearly as neutral during World War II as they liked to pretend. "Some day the truth will come out!"

In the living room Jane joined another group. She was standing closer to him now, and tipped her head back when she laughed. She laughed loudly. Every so often, she looked over at him and found his eyes already on her and her heart moved upward.

Yet he didn't come.

People began to leave.

At about ten o' clock she wandered over to a window and, cupping her hands around her eyes to block out the light, she looked up at the purple sky, the swaying branches, the large dark. Suddenly, the house seemed stifling and crowded. She went into the den and got her pea coat from the pile on the sofa and headed toward the door without smiling or waving or indicating in any manner that her departure deserved notice. Her boots scraped on the walk. It had become cold during the hours she'd been inside and she was glad, now, for her pea coat. She walked up the street toward the heath, past the glowing houses where people were doing whatever English things they did on a Thursday night, oblivious to the colonial holiday. Her nose began to run from the cold and she tilted her head back to check it; she was the type to carry tissues, or even handkerchiefs, but as she wished she weren't that type, she never did. She looked at the stars without much attention and finally wiped her nose on her sleeve. In the next instant she had an animal sense of fear and goose-flesh all over. There was a person just behind her. She'd heard no one approach. Everything inside her stopped.

There was a tap on her shoulder. She froze.

"I saw you leave," he said.

"You surprised me."

"Did I?" he asked knowingly.

She blushed. "Yes. Although I admit I hoped—"

"You hoped?"

"Um."

"Do you mean you hoped in general, or was there an object attached to it? I'm suspecting the latter. The circumstances of the day haven't been the sort conducive to hoping with nothing in mind."

"Maybe I *was* hoping for something."

"What?"

134

"You guess."

He propped one elbow in the palm of his other hand and stroked his jaw. "I think—now maybe I'm going out on a limb here, maybe I'm being presumptuous, maybe when I say this you're going to shoot me down like a tin can off a fence—but my guess is that you were hoping I'd do exactly what I did. That I'd follow you. At least that's what I hope you hoped."

A cat darted by.

"Well?" he prompted.

"I'm smiling," she said.

"So I'm right?"

"At least."

He gave a low chuckle that went through her coat and sweater and skin, into her. It only made sense for her to tip forward until her forehead rested against his chest. His arms came up around her, pulling the rest of her in. It was the first time she'd been with a man where she hadn't been able to crest his shoulder with her chin. She turned her head to the side so her cheek pressed against his lapel. She thought he'd kiss her, but he stayed still, quietly holding her, forcing a couple to step off the path and around them to go on. His buckskin jacket was open so she could hear his heart. He held his arms around her back, hard, then separated from her slightly, pushing and holding at the same time. Not letting her go—merely taking a step back so they could look at each other. He kept his hands on her shoulders and she took hold of his lapels.

"I know you," he said.

She nodded.

"I liked that corn pudding."

She had to kiss him. Couldn't wait.

She tugged on his lapels. He lowered his head. His mustache smelled of wine, but his mouth tasted of him. She kissed him hard and fervently, making herself perfectly clear, and she thought she should tell him that she wasn't always like this, in fact not ever; she wanted him to know this, not out of any petty concern that he might judge her morals, but so as to assure him of his vast value.

"I'm," she said, then took a breath. "Yours," she finished.

He touched her cheek.

"Is that all right?" she asked.

"That's a question for yourself, not for me."

"It is all right, then."

He brushed at her forehead, moving the hair aside and tucking it behind her ear. Was it really only this afternoon that she'd scribbled a poem about solitude? She hugged him around the waist so strenuously that he laughed.

"Whoa! Don't kill me."

"I want to pick you up!" She squeezed around his hips and lifted, but had no success. "I'll get stronger."

He found her hands and placed his palms against hers and moved them up between their chests. He kissed her, and already there was history in it. She knew his mouth, its warmth.

He looked at his watch. "I should get going if I'm going to make the last tube." He didn't move, though. "There're a few things you need to know," he said.

"I want to know everything, tonight!" She was exuberant.

"Jane, this is serious." He laid his hands on her shoulders. "I'm getting a divorce. I didn't even want to get married in the first place. I only did it because her parents offered us a car if we did. And we needed that car."

Jane said nothing. She tried to think.

"Say something."

"I'd hate it if someone described their marriage to me like that."

"I'm telling you the truth," he said.

"Did you love her?" Jane asked.

"I don't use that word—but that's another story. I cared about her, if that's what you mean. I still do. But we aren't lovers."

She understood. It sobered her to understand—the contours of the situation were adult in a way that she'd never before experienced—but she did. Clay and his wife weren't lovers. She and Clay were, after one kiss.

"I see."

"I wanted you to know, now. I didn't want you to hear it from someone else. That I'm still technically married."

"Thank you. I'm glad you told me."

The information had been a gift. It was only fair for her to offer one of her own.

"I know a shortcut," she said, and took the first step.

. . .

They woke up early, having slept hard and woven together in her nun's bed. "Would you like to take a walk?" he asked after breakfast.

"You read my mind," she said happily.

The temperature had dropped further overnight, and she ran back inside to get a scarf and gloves. She had an extra scarf for him, but nothing else she owned could possibly fit him.

"That's all right," he said. "My blood freezes at sixty degrees. Anything below that is all the same to me."

They walked for hours. He told her he liked to take a tube or a bus to the end of the line and bushwhack his way back relying solely on his sense of direction, without using a map.

"We'll do it soon," he said, affording a vision of a future. Jane already believed in one but was pleased to hear it referred to aloud.

That afternoon they did not take a bus or a tube but traveled on their feet. Clay didn't name a destination, and Jane wasn't curious after the first few minutes, when her curiosity was more perfunctory than genuine. She was content to walk beside him and watch the changing shape of their shadows as the sun lowered. They talked most of the time, and when they lapsed into silence, she tried to come up with a new subject.

"We can be quiet for a while, you know," he proclaimed when she asked him about his elementary school teachers. "It doesn't all have to happen today."

"It doesn't?" she asked, only half joking. *What if he dies tonight?* she wondered, her old, driving fear.

"I don't think so. Does it?"

"No. We have plenty of time," she said, and he swung her hand.

He told her about California, a tale very different than Colette's. He grew up in the Central Valley, outside Sacramento, in a town surrounded by lettuce fields. For as long as he could remember, he wanted to get away. His parents seemed like strangers. He was deeply relieved when they finally told him he was adopted—it gave him a way to make sense of them, at last—and he moved to San Francisco to celebrate. He didn't like San Francisco; too precious. On to L.A. He hadn't imagined while scuffling through the lettuce fields, skirting basking snakes, that any place could be so perfect. He loved L.A. so much that he'd applied for the job in London on purpose to give himself a break. He wanted to get away from his long, discursive drives around the city, which used up valuable writing time, but as travelers soon discover, he hadn't gotten away from himself. He'd substituted walking for driving. He was distracted by London, too.

"And now you," he said. "I'll be lucky if I write postcards."

"I'm a distraction, am I?"

"Yes. You, I think, are going to be the worst."

"Thanks. I think." In her naïveté Jane was pleased. "What about your marriage?"

"That was a distraction, too, but mostly it was a mistake. I take the blame for that. I don't believe in marriage. I thought that would make it easy for me to be married, but it didn't. It was a case of bad faith all around." He leaned close and bumped against her on purpose. "What's so funny?"

"These new philosophies. Colette believes you can control when you fall in love and who with. You don't believe in marriage. Not what I was expecting from England." She

139

looked up at him. "How can you not believe in marriage? It certainly exists."

"For myself, I mean."

"And your wife?"

"She said she agreed with me, but after a while she started wanting all the trappings. And she should have them, if that's what she wants. But it can't come from me."

"My parents had a very unhappy marriage. But I'm not sure I've given up."

"You'll figure it out. Plenty of time for that, too," he said.

She'd brought along her guidebook and her *London AZ*, but Clay scoffed at them. He had his own view of the city, and no use for anyone else's, especially not the fussy authors of the *Blue Guide*. His tour included a couple of pubs where he liked to go to hear music; Joe Orton's house on Noel Road, unmarked by the official brass plaque that commemorated other writers' houses in London, an omission Clay found as outrageous as Joe Orton himself; a favorite fish-and-chips shop; and Arsenal Stadium, where he liked to stand on the terraces and listen to the lads curse when the side faltered.

"Nope, not at all how I imagined England," she said as he led her down a grim, gray, lifeless street. She was as enchanted by his version of London as she'd been by her guidebook recommendations. More so, in some ways. His version seemed *real*.

They ended up, finally, in front of a Georgian house with a glossy black door and an equally glossy black rail coming off the side of the front steps, beyond which the sidewalk dropped off into a rectangular area next to the basement where the garbage cans were kept.

"Home sweet home," Clay said.

"Oh." Jane regarded it with a different attention than the other houses she'd seen all day. The whole block was a row of such houses, although this one was the most fixed up. The rest of them looked like party dresses at the end of a rough night. She was surprised that, of all of them, he lived in this one. He seemed more ruined, more disinclined to the material. Was he rich? She hadn't thought so. On the walk he'd been careful about spending. She placed her foot tentatively on the lowest step and looked around to see where he was. He was grinning at her with his arms crossed.

"No such luck." He pointed at the cellar steps. She didn't understand.

"I rent the dungeon," he said.

She was embarrassed, but he waved for her to follow. She clattered behind him down the spiral iron steps.

"I'm going to check the mail." He disappeared to the back of the flat. She heard him walk up the back steps and clomp down again. He smiled when he rejoined her and casually dropped an envelope on the table. Automatically, she scanned the words but was at the wrong angle to make anything of them. She spotted a pile of pages and thought it must be his book.

"You want a cup of tea?" he offered.

"Are you going to have one?"

"Yes. But I could make one for you even if I weren't."

He went to the galley kitchen on the far side of the room

and banged around. Water thundered from the tap into the kettle. He picked up a wrinkled old tea bag and put it in a cup. He took a second cup from the shelf and she read his mind as he wondered if he could use the ratty old tea bag for both cups, or should he spring for a fresh bag for the guest? She, in turn, wondered for the first time all day what she was doing with him. Suddenly, she felt quite separate from him, as if she could walk back out the door and think of him afterward only as a funny anecdote. One-night stand. The older novelist in London. She looked at him and saw flaws, his *de trop* height and a lozenge of pale scalp near his crown. Aging. Holes at his elbows. He was a stranger. She didn't mind having slept with him because sometimes it was preferable to sleep with strangers, no harm done there. But she had a strong feeling that she should stop now, this wasn't for her, it was all to do with Thanksgiving and homesickness, glamour and pity. Then he came to her proffering a steaming mug, and she saw his face and what she'd held in her arms in the night and the sense of strangeness vanished. He was a friend and he'd made her tea.

"Come on," he said, tilting his head for her to follow. "I'll give you the tour."

There were only two other rooms, and a loo. The spare bedroom was painted yellow, and there was an old-fashioned one-piece school desk with a paddle arm. Naturally, there were children's initials carved into the wood. Children always tried to make their mark.

"I like it," Jane said. "It's cozy."

"For a basement. Every so often Mrs. Kittredge asks me

upstairs to see what all the banging I've endured is about. I drink a cup of tea with Mrs. K., and then I get sent back down here—where, as you can see, not much interior design is happening at all. Except the bed. That was my idea. I'm proud."

"This bed?" It looked narrow, but normal. A cot.

"No. Mine. In the other room."

He took her teacup from her—she hadn't had any—and led her next door. Essentially, he'd tied two beds together with rope. The expanse of mattresses took up all of one room.

"Try it," he said.

She lay down and only understood the true nature of his suggestion when he settled beside her. She smiled to herself. He hadn't touched her all day beyond hand-holding and occasional pokings and proddings, and she'd begun to wonder, but now here he was; she knew where this was leading. She pretended to be oblivious and stared up at the small window cut into the wall at a height near the ceiling.

"I can see the sky," she said. "A slice of the sky. I feel like a prisoner. The *Bird Man of Alcatraz*."

He laced his fingers behind his head. He was taking his time; she wasn't used to that in a boy. But then, he wasn't a boy. She laced her fingers, too, with an ironic flourish, but he didn't notice the slight tease. His brow was furrowed; he was thinking.

"I used to want to be in prison," he said, "so I could be left alone to write. But then I found out they leave the lights on all night."

"I think that's actually the least of the inconveniences."

He looked over at her. She rolled onto her side and put a hand lightly on his chest.

"Tell me about your book," she said.

His tee shirt came loose of his pants and she saw a glimpse of his belly. Black fur. It made her want, like thirst. He shifted onto his side, causing her hand to slip to the mattress, where he covered it with his. He poked his thumb under her palm and worked it back and forth like a windshield wiper.

"Are you really thinking about my book?"

"I don't know. I'm not sure I'm thinking at all," she said.

"You must be thinking something. It's hard not to think. But it's even harder to think well."

He made her laugh. He was so strict. She could picture him as a child wondering what the teacher was talking about, not because he didn't understand but because the lesson seemed . . . no, he wouldn't say 'irrelevant.' *Spurious*, perhaps. Doubtless he had a feel for the spurious even before he knew the word. "Do you think I think well?" she asked.

"So far so good. I haven't heard you say anything stupid."

She cuffed him. He looked at his arm, where she'd struck, as if for blood. To further make his point, he rubbed it.

"Jeez, what would you do if I criticized you?"

"I'd probably believe you," she said.

He laughed. "Come here."

She moved onto his chest, but she wasn't done with the conversation. "I'd like you to read my poems," she said. "But the idea frightens me."

"I'd have to be honest."

"How did I already know that? That's the problem. I'd like you to read them and love them."

He smiled and played with her fingers. "Of course. That's what everyone wants. People come to my class thinking they want help, but what they're really after is praise. Affirmation more of self than of their prose. Whatever one writes is the best you can do at that moment. Good writing is good thinking. How can it not follow that a criticism of the writing is an implied criticism of much, much more?"

"I take it back. I don't want you to read them. Unless you let me read your book."

"I don't show my work to anyone until it's finished."

She considered this. It seemed smart. "I'd like to talk to you about writing, though."

He didn't respond.

"But not now," she said quickly.

"No," he agreed, putting his hand under her turtleneck. "Definitely not now."

. . .

It was dark when she got up again. She felt presumptuous from having thrilled him and didn't question that she was within her rights to rummage for a towel and step into the shower and let the hot water run past necessity, even if she were using it up. She washed her hair with his shampoo and her body with his soap, and her skin flushed beyond even all the scrubbing when she thought of how he'd touched her.

She brushed her teeth and made a few adjustments to her braid, and walked out of the bathroom in a mood of lusty triumph, ready to triumph again.

He wasn't in the bedroom. Nor the main room.

"Clay?" she called. No answer. "Clay?" Nothing. He was gone, completely, from every room; vanished. She pulled on her jeans and turtleneck and one of his big flannel shirts and went to the main room to wait. Surely he meant for her to wait. She picked up the book lying by his chair. Ronald Firbank. But she couldn't read; she was too happy to read, and too bereft—where was he? He could have left her a note, she thought. He had left her a note. There it was, on the writing table, propped up on the typewriter. He'd gone to get food. She was about to sit down with Firbank again when she noticed the envelope he'd collected earlier. She knew even before she read the return address that it was from *her*. She bent closer to look at the handwriting, and she needed no help from Colette to recognize the style, to know what kind of girl made her letters that way, blocky and clear with no attempt at embellishment or to make an impression. A hockey player. Good at science. The kind of girl to whom nothing bad had happened. Whose entire depth came from her faith that everything would work out for the best.

Not like me, Jane thought.

Something was happening to her now. To Mrs. West, that was. But was it bad? It couldn't be. Clay wouldn't hurt anyone.

When Clay returned, he found her sitting in the child's desk, writing on a yellow tablet.

"What are you working on?" he asked.

She covered the page with her forearm. "A poem. But I'm stuck."

"Fish and chips will help."

They went back into the living room. Mrs. West's letter still lay on the table. She was glad he had nothing to hide.

. . .

Colette was sitting on her doorstep when she got home.

"How long have you been here?"

"Nearly half a pack. I'm dying of curiosity. I need the whole story over a drink. Or two."

On their way down the hill, Jane marveled at how Colette's velvet cape paled from the cold. Her own lungs felt lined with ice crystals. Because it was the first cold day of the season, though, and not a bitter insult in a long line of many, she was excited by it. She was happy with the scrubbed soreness between her legs; her body felt properly employed. Wanton.

"Hey!" Colette's arm was like the stop signal across a railroad track. "Did you see that?"

"What? What was it?"

"That was George Harrison!"

Jane looked down the road at the disappearing car. It was low to the ground and sporty and black and reminded her of the facts that she knew about George from *16* magazine; that he loved avocados and Jaguar X-KEs. She had loved him. She still wore espadrilles all summer because of how he'd looked in them in *Help!* For years she'd believed if only they could meet, she'd be made somehow happy. She'd believed it way beyond the moment when the other girls had put their Beatle souvenirs in the attic or the trash. Now she'd had her chance, and she'd missed it. She searched herself for regret, but all she found was tranquility. She no longer needed him. "Oh well."

"That's all you can say? Your idol, and you didn't even see him? You," she said, poking a leather-covered finger into Jane's pea coat, "you really are a goner!"

Jane nodded. She was.

ON VALENTINE'S DAY, Jane walked from her flat down to Camden Town to pick up the sheaf of poems she'd left at the print shop the previous afternoon. It was a long, cold walk; the stiff cuffs of her jeans cut at her ankles and her eyes streamed. She wasn't thinking of her discomfort, however. She was trying to figure out a way to celebrate a holiday with a man who, on principle, didn't believe in holidays or celebration. She'd managed Christmas by decorating his flat with the top of a tree someone had left on the street and hanging it with singles he liked. The Specials. X-Ray Spex. Elvis Costello. Ultravox. She bought him an old record player in a resale shop, and he was so pleased with the presents that he didn't rail too much against the tradition. He even willingly accompanied her to Nigel and Colette's for Christmas dinner, a long bacchanal that threaded one meal into three and rendered them so knackered that they slept in the guest room rather than walking back to her flat. When they returned to his place on the afternoon of Boxing Day, he gave her her presents, explaining that he hadn't wanted to give them to her on Christmas Day, because where would be the surprise in that? He gave her books. They were not books she'd have picked for herself—Handke, Kleist, Orton—but she was happy to have them. She asked him to inscribe them to her.

"Why should I write in them? The authors already did. Isn't that enough?"

He amused her with his pronouncements. He was so opposed to doing anything that an ordinary person might do. It was Clay against the world and everyone in it—except for her. Her exemption from his usual judgments and censure sometimes unnerved her—surely the day would come when she'd slip up—but she couldn't help but be complimented. She only wished she knew—why her? When she asked him, he said it was because she didn't try to impress people.

"I might, if I knew how," she said.

"Exactly my point."

She was no clearer about what she was doing right, but apparently it worked, and that had to be enough. She of all people understood it was impossible to have everything.

She stopped in a shop and bought a bottle of wine. She'd seduce him, she decided, pure and simple. That was a celebration he wouldn't mind. Afterward they'd eat and she'd give him her poems.

It began to snow lightly. The dry flakes accumulated on her pea coat, and she didn't brush them off. In all her fantasies while she was growing up, she'd never imagined falling in love in the winter. Yet winter was perfect. What better than a dusky afternoon in bed?

Her ideas, too, had been wrong about how she'd feel when

she loved somebody. She'd thought it would be like having a twin, a soul mate with whom she'd communicate by telepathy, but it was larger than that, and far more complicated. She'd thought she'd felt alone before, but it was nothing compared to her sense of isolation when they argued. The communion, though, was sublime. But she wasn't allowed to tell him. He'd been serious when he said he didn't believe in talking about love. It had been odd, at first, when she'd wanted to say so much, but it had become a discipline, and very much like her old fantasies of stalwart reticence. Occasionally, she succumbed to the temptations of conventional chat. Once when they were going to a party, she asked if she looked all right.

"You know you're pretty," he said. "You don't need me to tell you."

"It would be nice."

"Puppies and kittens are *nice*. Not me."

He is nice, though, she thought as she entered the High Street. People generally liked him once they got past his posturing and bluster. True, he was pretentious, and arrogant, but he was also very sweet. Even Colette saw his good points; they spent hours talking about how much they missed bear claws and Mexican food and other L.A. specialties. Jane wondered, from time to time, how he'd fit in in Wynnemoor. She guessed he'd find a way, if it came to that. She knew he'd never want to live there. She also knew that was one of the things she liked about him. He wouldn't lead her backward.

She was nervous about showing him her poems. Nigel had

shown her copies of several of Clay's stories that the class had scouted out here and there. They were like nothing she'd ever read before; bleak, but in a way that suggested a great disappointment rather than pure cynicism. She reread them until she had parts memorized that stayed with her all the time. She'd tried to discuss them with Clay, but he looked so pained at the mention of them that she let it go.

She learned from him in spite of himself, by his example. He showed her, in the way he lived, what it took to accomplish serious work. She saw him sit for twelve hours straight, and in that time accumulate only half a page of words. She saw him rip pages up.

"If there's anything worth saving, I'll think of it again," he said.

"How do you know?"

"I don't. But I always think of something, so I can't prove myself wrong."

It scared her to throw pages away, especially when there were lines she liked. Yet she found that she, too, always thought of something. She had a growing sense of abundance. They'd have a good night, in spite of his opposition to fiestas.

A bell chimed when she opened the door of the shop. A man came out from the back. It was Gavin.

"Hi," she said.

"Hello, Jane. You want your poems, I expect."

She nodded.

He reached down under the counter and pulled the packet

up. She'd asked for three sets, to be on the safe side. "Here they are. They're good, you know."

"You read them?"

"I recognized the name, and it hasn't been a very busy day. I was wondering if I'd ever see you again. I thought maybe you'd gone home by now. I take it you haven't been lonely."

He tipped his head toward the poems.

"Look, Gavin, I'm sorry about that night. I tried to say goodbye, but I couldn't get near the stage."

"You tried to say goodbye?"

"I wanted to."

"I thought you left with someone."

"With Colette."

He slapped his forehead with his palm.

"I didn't know how to find you," Jane said. "You never came back to the house."

"Pride, pride." He shook his head. "I suppose it's too late now?"

She nodded.

"Too bad." He crossed his arms. "I'd like to inspire a girl to write poems like that. They'd make good lyrics. Have you ever thought of writing for a band?"

"I've never shown them to anyone. You're the first person who's read them."

"So what are you going to do with them?"

"Do?" The shop was cold. Gavin was wearing two sweaters.

"Where are you going to send them?"

"I'm not going to send them anywhere. They're for my—friend. A surprise, for Valentine's Day."

"But they should be published."

"Do you really think they're good enough?"

"I read lots," he said, "and these are better than most. The best since Sylvia Plath, I'd say, in the women."

"Thanks. I think."

She was taken aback. And interested.

"You shouldn't waste these on just one man. They should be in a magazine."

"What magazine?" she asked.

"I don't know. Where would you like them to be published?"

"The *New Yorker.*"

"All right. That's where you'll send them."

"They'll never be accepted there."

"You know that for sure, do you? Are you psychic, then?"

In England, "then" often meant "now," perhaps because it was a country obsessed with merging the past with the present. The opposite of me, Jane thought.

"Why don't you write me a lyric, to make up for my broken heart?"

"I'll think about it." Jane tucked the poems in her knapsack. "How much do I owe you?"

"Get out of here. Go write me a song. You'd be glad you did when we're famous."

"Maybe I'll be the famous one."

She felt him watch her as she walked out the door.

. . .

Nigel looked more disheveled than she'd ever seen him, but just as attractive. What was it about loose, rumpled shirt-tails? "Hello, hello," he said. "I hope you've come to be my Valentine."

"Definitely." She leaned to kiss him on the cheek.

"Um. That felt nice." Charmingly, he touched the spot. "Come in. Colette's not here, but she shouldn't be long."

"Actually, I've come to see you. I need your advice."

"I was working. On a story."

"Oh, I'm sorry." She took a step backward. "I don't want to interrupt . . ."

He reached for her arm and pulled her in. "Did you see how quickly I answered the door?"

She smiled. "I'm so used to Clay. He'd gladly kill anyone who interrupts him."

"Even you?"

"Probably. I've never tested it. Where do you work, any-way?" she asked. "In your room?" She'd never seen his bed-room. He kept the door closed.

He stopped abruptly. She couldn't see his face, but she felt his hesitation. "Never mind. Clay works in the living room, so I'm used to it being a public spectacle. In my flat I work in the only room, while looking out the window—"

He held up his hand to stop her.

"I'm chattering, aren't I?"

"It's all right. I'll show you." He gestured for her to re-move her coat and lay it over the bannister.

"No. I don't want to invade your privacy."

"Come on, before I change my mind."

They walked upstairs, passing Colette's room, the guest room, all the way to the end of the hall, to the door that was always shut. He opened it, and she gaped. "It's beautiful." The room was open, with its minimal furniture placed in unexpected spots and nothing at all on or near the walls except paint. She walked the circumference. It was decorated up to the top of the dado, which was also painted. She was in a garden under a navy sky. "I'm in heaven," she said.

"My mother taught me how to draw flowers."

"These don't look very English. More tropical."

"My fantasy life. I liked the Gauguin scenery."

"How long did this take?"

"Not long. A couple of weeks. I stayed up."

"I always wanted a room painted this way." A thought occurred to her. "You did all the decorating downstairs, too, didn't you? It was you, not Colette."

"I neither confirm nor deny." He spoke with bravado, but he clasped his hands like a schoolboy behind his back.

"I haven't paid attention," she said.

"I didn't ask for it."

"I apologize."

"No need. We are here, now. Things happen when they should."

He showed her to a gray wicker chaise. He sat on the end.

"So do you think people are fated to meet each other?" she asked.

He grinned. "How are things with you and Clay?"

She sighed. "Am I that obvious?"

"Colette is waiting for you to come back down to earth."

"Colette doesn't believe he's really getting a divorce. She thinks it's meaningful that Clay hasn't said he loves me."

"Hasn't he?"

"He doesn't believe in it."

"Why am I not surprised?"

He went to the desk in the middle of the room and came back with a piece of paper. She saw it was the first page of a story. Across the top were written the words *cut all references to "love" and this will be decent.* Jane recognized that angry, exacting sensibility. It was the one to which her references to love—no quotes—had become attached. She and Nigel grinned at each other.

"What can you do?" she said.

"Colette is a romantic. You have to weigh that in."

Jane was shocked. "A romantic? But she's such a realist. She's skeptical of his intentions. And protective of me."

"She's skeptical of his claims. She doesn't consider people's intentions. That's the ultimate in romanticism." He took the paper back and clipped it to a manuscript. "She's jealous, too," he said, "in case you didn't know."

Now she was sure he was off track. Colette liked Clay, but only as a friend.

"She has nothing to be jealous about," she said.

"You're in a relationship and she isn't."

"But she doesn't want one! She wants to marry you."

Nigel turned his back to her and took a few steps away. "That's the trouble," he said quietly.

"What is?"

He turned back around. "Nothing. Forget it, I'm in a mood. We were talking about you, and Clay. What do you think? Do you trust him?"

Jane had asked herself this, and gave him her conclusion. "I have to. If I don't, I have to stop."

"Well, then. What does it matter what anyone else thinks?"

"Colette's not just anyone."

"True." He seemed about to say more, but changed the subject. "Anyway. You had a question."

"Oh." Her purpose seemed far away. "I wanted an opinion on some poems. Someone told me I should send them out."

"Sure," he said easily. "Let's make it even. I just finished a new story. Trade?"

"Does it contain any love?"

"You'll see."

He handed her a pile of handwritten pages and settled on his bed to read hers. She looked down at his manuscript but soon drifted; on the occasions that she'd expressed insecurity, had Colette encouraged it? No, she decided, it was disloyal to even consider it. She began to read again, then glanced up to catch Nigel's expression as he reacted to her poems. His poker face told her nothing; nor did he look at her, which made her self-conscious of doing the opposite. Finally, she read in earnest. The story was set at a posh public school and concerned a boy who was picked on for being different. She lingered over the last page as she tried to decide what to say. She felt her face grow hot, and hoped it didn't show.

"Who first?" he asked.

"I don't care." Clay had never told her about Nigel's writing. She'd assumed it was good. Colette was so convinced about him.

"In that case, you tell me. And Jane. I want the truth."

She nodded, miserable, remembering what Clay had said about writers never wanting to hear the truth.

"I mean it," Nigel said.

"All right. But this is only my opinion, remember."

"That's what I want."

She laid the pages on her knees. "I think it's not like this room. This room, this house—everything's in the right place. It's artless, and beautiful." She glanced over at the walls. "Your painting is so free. I can't get over how good it is."

"And the story isn't."

"I wouldn't say that. There are good moments and observations, but overall it feels . . . squashed."

"Squashed."

She felt goosebumps rise on her arms. Perhaps she'd been wrong, and shouldn't have taken him at his word. But it was too late to back off now. "It feels as though you're holding back. There's something you want to say, but you're not saying it. And the holding back affects everything—the writing, the structure, all of it."

He raised his hands to his face.

"Nigel?" She was horrified—had she made him cry?

"Go on," he said through his fingers. His shoulders vibrated.

She felt queasy. "I do think there are many good parts. The whole thing could be good, with a little more work. You certainly have talent. God, Nigel."

She went to him, put her arm around him. It was awful to feel the way he shook.

"Jane, Jane, Jane." He dropped his arms. To her surprise, he was laughing. Laughing! "It's okay. Really. You don't know the favor you've done me. Believe me, you said all the right things."

"I did?"

He smelled of sandalwood. It must be the soap of the month, plucked from the basket in the bathroom downstairs. People who came to the at homes often brought soaps as gifts.

"I promise. I've been wanting to hear that. I was waiting for someone to tell me. You didn't say anything that I don't think myself."

"What does Clay say?"

Nigel considered this. "Now that I think about it, he says pretty much the same, actually. He puts it differently, though."

"How?"

Nigel imitated him. "'Why the hell should I give a ruddy rat's ass about these effete assholes?'"

Jane smiled. "Not to put too fine a point on it."

"I've been trying to answer that question, writing this

same stupid thing over and over. But now I know the right way to handle it."

"Honestly?"

"Honestly. I see the light, thanks to you. I wish I'd shown it to you sooner." He left the bed and walked to a drinks tray that stood at such a distance from any other furnishing that it took on a sculptural aura; he poured them both a glass of Scotch. "You're a friend indeed, Jane." They clinked. "To not holding back," he said.

"I second that."

They sat companionably on the chaise.

"How's your uncle?" he asked.

"Francis?"

"Is he coming back soon?"

"I don't know." It took her a moment to remember that Francis had offered to help Nigel find a job. She worried that Francis hadn't meant it, and that Nigel was sitting in this amazing room, painting his beautiful murals, counting on an offhand remark made at a party. "Shall I write him and ask?"

They heard the door open and close downstairs.

"Colette's back. We should go down." He shoved his hands into his pockets. "Maybe you could give me his address?"

"Sure. I'll bring it by tomorrow."

They stood up. Colette called from below.

"Coming," they said at the same time.

"But we never talked about your poems," he said.

"That's okay. I don't really think they're ready to send out, anyway."

"But you have to. I loved them. They're so sexy. I *knew* you were sexy!"

I didn't, she thought. A few months ago she knew nothing about it.

"You really think they're good enough?" She picked them up off the quilt.

"Uh-oh. Don't start acting like a real writer."

"You're right. Forget I said that. And thank you. I'm going to do it. Why not?"

"Exactly."

Via had once said that no child of hers was going to be ambitious. *Ambition is a dirty word*, she'd proclaimed. But Jane had become sexy and ambitious, and lightning hadn't struck yet.

They met Colette on the second-floor landing. She smelled of the cold.

"I just bought scones and crème fraîche. What have you two been up to?"

"Waiting for you," Nigel said. "Jane needs your opinion."

Colette's eyes gleamed. Those were some of her favorite words.

. . .

Jane followed Colette's instructions for including a return envelope in the mailing. Colette knew about such things. She walked Jane to the post office and supervised the stamping so Jane couldn't lose her nerve. Jane turned to leave, but Colette surprised her by walking up to the window.

"I have a little something to mail myself." She displayed

the envelope. It was addressed to Lady Georgina Kirby-Kerr.

Jane grabbed Colette's arm. "Nigel's mother?"

"The very same. It's time we begin a correspondence." She pushed the letter across the counter and paid for the posting.

"Does Nigel know?"

"In general terms. We've been talking about the future." She linked arms with Jane and they walked outside. The snow had stopped, and the air felt scrubbed. Hampstead looked like a country village. "I think we should have a big wedding, after all. If we don't, considering his position, it may not look respectable. It takes time to plan such events."

"Clay and I never talk about the future. He doesn't want to until he finishes his novel. He's afraid it would distract him too much."

"That's all right. Let him work. Meanwhile, you make the plans."

"How can I do that without him?"

"Believe me, it would be harder to do it with him."

Jane laughed. Colette had a way of putting things.

"You decide what's going to happen, and when the time is right, you tell him."

"Tell Clay?"

"He won't notice. He's a man, isn't he? You just make it seem as though it was something you discussed."

"I don't think that would work with him. Anyway, that isn't what I want."

"You want to marry him, don't you?"

"Not necessarily marry. I want us to be partners." Jane thought of what Nigel had said. "Does that bother you?"

"Why would it?"

"I don't know. You wanted me to focus on my work."

"You are, though. Your poems are great! No, I'm counting on us being fat matrons together. We're going to lie in bed and eat bonbons. And by the way, you're going to be my maid of honor."

"I'm not going to have to wear something awful, am I?"

"Would I allow an awfully dressed maid of honor at my wedding? Remember who you're talking to, please."

"I wish I could be there when you meet his mother."

"All I'll have to do is convince her that I've gotten Nigel to change his ways and I'm made in the shade. Then it's the country life for me—punctuated by a few trips here and there, of course. Better yet, a few houses."

Impulsively, Jane hugged her. In some ways she was more involved with Colette than with Clay. There was a greater pressure on the intimacy between them because they didn't have sex to do the work; and then they had the strangeness of sameness to intrigue them.

"What was that for?" Colette asked.

"Valentine's Day. And because you're the greatest friend I've ever had."

"You, too, Jane. When I'm rich, I'm going to buy you a whole new wardrobe. In the meantime, I need some cigs."

They went into an off-license where, within seconds, Colette managed to get into an argument with the Pakistani proprietor about the price of Marlboros. What was Nigel thinking of when he claimed she was a romantic?

. . .

Clay was silent for a disturbingly long time. Jane monitored him as she wiped out the kitchen sink. Finally, he laid the poems on his lap.

"Interesting."

"You're welcome."

She undid the sash of her robe, which was all she'd put on after taking a shower. She walked with aplomb to his chair, inviting him to watch her. Then she realized what she'd said, and blushed. "You know what I mean." She brushed her knees against his. "I sent them out today."

It excited her for him to be fully dressed while she was nearly naked. She'd found it a never ending source of surprise to learn what excited her; it seldom was what she'd heard about or seen in magazines.

"You did? To where?"

"The *New Yorker*."

He pulled his head back with a swift, disapproving jerk. "Why would you do that?"

She continued her knee play, but with less conviction. "Why not?"

"Because. You just started writing. Why would you even think the *New Yorker* might publish you?"

"I don't know. Beginner's luck?"

"Not a good idea, Jane. They keep records. If you send

them something that isn't good, they won't be in any hurry to read whatever you send the next time. You go to the bottom of the pile. It's a good way to blow your chances permanently."

She looked at him, wondering if he realized what he'd just implied about her poems. Her love poems. He was rubbing his forehead with his long fingers, looking across the room toward the Specials poster. She took a step backward and closed her robe.

"I can't do anything about it now, I already mailed them," she said.

He shrugged. "Oh well." He leaned to the side and picked up his book. Nabokov. He opened it to the marked page and held it at reading distance.

"Never mind about that," she said quickly. "What do you think about them?" She hoped she sounded calmer than she felt. She didn't want to argue. It was Valentine's Day.

He flipped forward a page, and then back again. "They're pretty good," he said without looking up.

"I hoped they'd make you happy."

"Happy?"

"Yes. I wrote them for you, not the *New Yorker*. I only sent them because . . . I don't know why. It's what you're supposed to do, isn't it?" She thought better of telling him she'd shown them to Colette and Nigel.

He folded the book around his index finger to keep his place marked. His other hand beat a rhythmic pattern on top of his leg. "There are hundreds of other journals aside from the *New Yorker*."

"I know."

"I could have made some suggestions. I have relationships with several editors."

Had she somehow insulted him? "It was an impulse. I don't expect anything to come of it. It was just fun to send them, to think of them landing on someone's desk in New York."

"Fun, eh? I can't even remember the last time I thought of writing as fun. If I ever did."

"You're making me feel foolish."

"If the shoe fits—"

She kicked him, astonishing them both. She was further amazed to find she wasn't sorry.

"Jane, I was *kidding*."

"Oh. And am I foolish for not realizing that?" She was shaking.

He leaned forward and reached his hand toward her. She moved out of range. "Jane, Jane, honestly. The last thing I think of you as being is foolish. I was just playing. What I said was completely dull-witted. I'm the foolish one. I haven't made you understand how good these poems really are."

She had a fleeting awareness of the authority he claimed for himself of being the arbiter of her work's value. It also occurred to her that he was placating her. She wasn't used to seeing him harshly, however, and backed away from it.

"Really?"

"Really. They show talent. You're a genius compared to my students."

"Then do you think my poems have a chance?"

"A chance? There's always a chance. But I wouldn't get your hopes up. *I* haven't been published in the *New Yorker*. They're too mainstream for my work. Too East Coast establishment." He shrugged. "But you never know. Anyway, thank you for them. May I keep them?"

His beseeching tone recast the feeling between them. She took the book out of his hand—careful to mark his place—and picked up the poems, then sat down on his lap and embraced him. "I told you, they're for you."

He took the sheaf back from her and began to scan the top page. "They could stand some editing. I could show you a few things."

She accepted that without bristling. He was the real writer, after all. "That's what I was hoping."

He saw her legs, and the gaping robe.

"You were, were you?" He put his hand between her breasts.

"Happy Valentine's Day."

"The *New Yorker* will be foolish if it doesn't publish those poems."

"Tell me more," she said, but soon made that impossible.

LOOK AT THIS," Colette said, gesturing to take in the sweep of the landscape. "Wouldn't you love it if this were your private property?"

They were walking through Hyde Park after having eaten lunch at the Hard Rock Cafe; every so often Colette broke her exacting culinary rules for a cheeseburger and fries. It was May, and warm. For the past few weeks Jane had walked around the city touching the tips of her fingers to buds and unfurling leaves. That morning she'd pulled her espadrilles out of the closet.

"I can't imagine it," Jane said.

"I can. I'd have no problem owning half of London. But Nigel's place will have to do."

She'd gone down to meet his family, and came back transformed. The punk regalia was out. Bond Street and ladies' shops in Knightsbridge were in. She kept her eyes open for her new ilk—Sloane Rangers, they were called, Sloane Square being their home base—and copied their clothes and makeup. Although she'd only go so far. She'd told Jane to kill her if she ever had the insane notion to wear a Peter Pan collar. To Jane's consternation, Colette had begun to look like her old schoolmates from Wynnemoor. In fact, not unlike Jane herself.

"I can't wait to see it."

"We'll all go down this summer for a house party. I'm going to have lots of them, and invite every celebrity I've ever wanted to meet. Directors, too, and, more importantly, producers. I'll invite George Harrison for you."

"I don't want to meet him. I don't need to meet him."

"Maybe he needs to meet you. Did you ever think of that?"

Jane recalled the game she'd played with Susan Roberts in which they'd pretended John and George were their brothers. The lads needed their little sisters with them at all times, even at press conferences and especially on tour. The memory made her smile. "I did, actually. But not anymore."

"Tough. You're going to meet him anyway. I'm hoping to stay there for a month while I finish my script and pick out china patterns. That's just an expression, by the way. They have enough china already to sink a small ocean liner. I hate gold plate, don't you?"

"So you've been working on your movie?"

"Of course. What's the point of being rich without being famous?"

"But that's great! You finished the script?"

"Just about. Let me tell you the opening. Close your eyes."

Jane looked around at the cars whizzing down Park Row and the hefty crowd walking in both directions on the sidewalk. "Now?"

"Just for a minute. Stop."

Jane did as she asked, aware of the glances shot their way. Any judgment they contained fell short of her. She'd learned to appreciate the freedom in being a crazy American.

Colette moved close to her ear. "Okay. So the screen is dark. Completely black. You hear a cello playing, and all you see is an orange light moving around. It looks like a firefly, and it's moving in some kind of synch with the music, but you can't quite put it together how. As you're watching this, the credits are rolling. They're in the same orange color as the light but they're on the lower right-hand corner of the screen so they don't interfere with the visual. This goes on for a couple of minutes, and then slowly the light comes up to reveal first the cello, and then the person who's playing it. He's a young guy, kind of punky, not who you'd expect to see playing the kind of music he's playing. You notice he's holding a cigarette in his bow hand. The tip of the cig is the light you've been seeing all along." She tapped Jane on the shoulder. "You can open your eyes now. It'll be like this, see?" She lit a cig and swirled it in the air. "So what do you think?"

"I think it's powerful. And very you. Then what happens?"

Colette began walking again. When Jane didn't instantly follow suit, Colette gestured impatiently for her to keep up. "Oh, you know. It's a coming-of-age story."

"So he's a teenager?"

"Or early twenties. Anyway, I better stop talking about it. You know what they say, that if you talk a story out too much it can be so satisfying that you never write it."

Jane nodded. No one's creative process was as fraught as

Clay's, and she'd learned how to handle that. Duck and cover.
As for her own, she was feeling her way. She did think she was
improving. As promised, Clay had shown her a few tricks.
"I'm ready to read it as soon as you're ready to show it."

"I know. I wish my hair would grow out more quickly. I'm
eating gelatin up the wazoo."

They were headed in the direction of Hyde Park Corner
and Buckingham Palace. Colette felt a personal connection
to it now. She was already planning what she'd wear to her
first garden party.

"Speaking of owning vast estates, I'm going to run out of
money soon," Jane said. "I'll have to give up my flat."

"Then you'll move in with us. Or can't Clay squeeze you
in? What's that big bed for, anyway?"

"I guess he'll be leaving, too. His job ends in June."

"Is he going back to California?"

Jane shrugged. There was a crowd gathered a few hundred
yards down the road. Jane took note of the long row of bobbies standing side by side, their black metal hats gleaming.

"Don't you think you have a right to know?"

"Yes. Yes, I do. But he won't talk about it. It has nothing to
do with me, it's just his policy. You know how he is."

"Then you have to give him an ultimatum. If he doesn't
make a firm plan by a certain date, you're going to stop seeing him."

Jane shook her head. "I can't do that."

"Why not?"

A brass band started up, sounding a distant triumph. The

warmth of the day seemed to render the notes round and mellow. "You've really never felt like this about anybody?"

Colette ignored her question. "You're not willing to give him an ultimatum, but you want to find out what his plans are. Then the question becomes, how are you going to go about getting the information you need?"

Jane wondered when Colette would be open about herself. It did no good to push her. "I don't know. But I bet you're going to tell me."

"If only you'd do as I say. I'd no idea you were so stubborn when I met you."

"I'm not stubborn!"

"You haven't taken a single piece of my advice. You've insisted on doing things your own way. What would you call that?"

"Wise?"

"Ha-ha." Colette rolled her eyes to the sky and turned up her palms. "All my expertise. For what?"

Jane didn't point out the incongruity of Colette having expertise on a subject about which she claimed no interest. Then again, being in love hadn't helped Jane become more proficient. Help could come from strange places.

"I'll listen now," she said.

Colette smiled. "That's more like it." Colette took her triumph in stride, without gloating. "If you don't want to confront him directly, you're going to have to be devious."

Jane wanted to disagree but checked the impulse.

"It's really just a math problem," Colette went on. She warmed to her subject, her hands forming French arabesques. "How do you find x?"

"You tell me. If I knew—"

"Think."

In fact, Jane had already thought about it. "It's getting awfully late. He must have some inkling by now. If he's going to teach again next year, he'd have to have applied for another job already."

"*Exactement oui.* So how could you find that out?"

"I don't know."

"I'll give you a hint. Where does he keep his mail?"

So that was where this was going. Well, she'd asked for it. "I'm not reading his mail, so forget it."

Colette rolled her eyes upward; she often gave the impression that she counted an all-knowing goddess as her confidante. "You're too uptight to read his mail, but you can wait to find out what he's going to be doing this June until he's ready to talk with you about it? You can live totally according to his timetable?"

They'd drawn close to the crowd. It was larger than it looked from far off. The bobbies no longer gave the impression of a receiving line. They were a barricade. Jane took it in without discernment. "Respecting other people's privacy is *uptight?*"

Colette didn't register the protest. "What's this all about?" There was apparently a scene ahead, some sort of a gathering.

"I don't know." Jane registered their surroundings only peripherally. Had he applied for a job? He often said he missed California. But he liked London, and he was curious about New York. Would he ask her to go with him? Would she, just like that? Just to be with him? Colette was right; she'd put herself in a vulnerable position.

"Did you hear anything about a holiday? I didn't."

Colette picked up speed and strode to the back of the crowd, with Jane following. No one was able to tell her precisely what was going on; one person said it was a National Front rally, another claimed it was an appearance by the Japanese ambassador. Exasperated, Colette turned to Jane. "Fuck this. Let's go to Harrod's."

They'd begun to turn around when there was a split-second change in the atmosphere, a rearrangement of energy that pulled the air away from them, as if it were being sucked up by a huge straw. They intuitively knew it presaged disaster, but before they could respond a booming noise shook the earth. When the echo died away seconds later, Jane was still standing, but the people closer to the explosion had been thrown to the ground. Further ahead fire spurted. The arc of bobbies dispersed and ran in all directions. Slowly—it was all slow, for the first second—the screaming began, scattered voices at first and then a mass, like sheep running over a cliff. There was panic in those voices, panic more than pain.

"This way!" Colette waved frantically.

Jane hesitated, feeling as though she should do something. She looked toward the blast. Some of the bobbies had formed a new circle now; in its center she saw, beneath a copse of flames, a ruined, burning car. No one inside it could possibly be alive.

"Come on," Colette said, grabbing her. "Let's get out of here."

Jane couldn't stop staring at the pyre. An intense pressure rose from her lungs to her throat, pinning her to the spot.

"Jane!" Colette snapped. "Are you deaf?"

A sound emerged from her, a low, dark hum that began inside her ribs and rose like a siren, until she screamed a brief, harsh blast. Her cry was only one of many, and immediately blended into all the other noise in the park. Within an instant it was gone, and people brushed by, oblivious, eager to save themselves. Only Colette had noticed, and she jerked around, startled. "Jane?"

Jane was shaking. The sound of her own voice vibrated in her inner ear and her lungs ached.

"I'm all right. Give me a minute." She wrapped her arms around her stomach and leaned forward to catch her breath. Her teeth chattered as if she were freezing.

"I'm not sure we have a minute," Colette said uneasily.

"All right. I'm coming."

They headed back up Park Row in a surging crush of bodies. Official vehicles flashed by, dozens of them, with their lights and sirens and horns whirling and bleating at full blast. Jane smelled smoke.

"They've closed the tube!" someone shouted, and the information spread through the crowd.

"Fuck," Colette said. "We're going to have to walk. And

these boots weren't made for walking, that's for damn sure."

Jane was pliant from shock, and deferred to Colette to get them home. It was lucky that she had such a competent guide, because her attention wasn't in the moment. Instead it was in the past, back when her life had changed from one thing to another, and she'd lost not only a father and a family, but also her innocence and her capacity to take anything for granted.

She barely listened to Colette's ongoing monologue, and didn't question their route until Colette led her into a Marks & Spencer.

"I hope they have sneakers here," Colette said. "I can't bring myself to call them 'trainers.' And let's get some cheese."

"Cheese? What about the people who were wounded? Here we are, and they're in the hospital."

Colette was unfazed. "There were people in the hospital before, and you weren't upset about them."

That wasn't true, though. Jane was upset. There was a part of her that was always upset, always aware of sorrow and death, that never let her completely forget that whatever good time she was having was apt to be snatched away in an instant.

After Emlin died, she'd played a game in bed at night of traveling to every continent in the world and witnessing horror; beatings of animals and children, murders, war. Sometimes she drove herself close to crazy, but her fantasies were still preferable to thinking about what had happened on the Schuylkill Expressway on a snowy February night, when an exhausted, heartbroken doctor drove through a guard rail and smashed dozens of feet below, his car exploding and his body melting to the point where there was nothing for the coffin except shards of bone and tooth. That was the core of her sorrow, and it was unbearable. If only she'd agreed to go out to dinner with him rather than watching the Beatles. If only she hadn't shown him that the phone was off the hook. In London she'd worked hard to stave off the grief, but it came back easily; it was her strong breaststroke, her hands-free balance on a bicycle. It was with her no matter where she went. Ghosts could cross water, after all.

Colette picked up a handbag and turned to Jane for an opinion. When she saw Jane's expression, she scowled. "Jane, are you going to be like this all day?"

Forever, she thought. "I'm sorry. I guess I'm funny about bombs."

"You don't have a very funny way of showing it."

"You wanted me to express my negative emotions."

"Not to *me*."

Colette was serious, which, in spite of everything, made Jane laugh.

. . .

Jane took a bath, then lay on the soft bed in Colette's guest room, trying to nap. Instead she remembered, over and over, the bomb going off, and shuddered at how close they'd come to harm. She looked at the ceiling and the lengthening shadows with the marvel of a survivor. Colors seemed brighter, bird calls more vivid and extraordinary. She raised her arms into the air and let her wrists drift to the left, then the right. She wished Clay didn't have a class that evening. She wanted to talk.

When she heard a chair scrape in Colette's room, she went and knocked on the door.

"*Entrez.*"

"Am I interrupting?" Jane stepped in, lifting her feet to avoid a pile of sweaters. She sat on the bed.

"Just the opposite. I was wondering when you'd surface. I'm completely antsy. Let's go out." Colette began to flick hangers along the rack of her heavy wardrobe. "Borrow anything you want."

"I love you, Colette. You know that, don't you?"

"I love you, too. How about this?" She pulled out a black dress with a scrolled lace top. The silky skirt swung freely.

Jane wasn't finished. "You and Nigel mean so much to me. I always wanted a happy family, and I feel like I have one now. I want you to know that, to say it out loud, because life can change so quickly. We never know how much time we have with anyone. I think it's important to say what you feel, so that if something happens, there won't be any regrets."

"*Je ne regrette rien.* That's my policy." Colette hung the dress on the wardrobe door and began rifling further.

"I wish I felt that way, but I don't. I never have. There are so many things I wish I'd said to my father. There are things I wish I hadn't done."

"You were a child."

"I know. I know that's supposed to absolve me of responsibility. But it doesn't change the way I feel."

"Which is?"

"Guilty.

"Guilt's a waste of time. But I doubt I could talk you out of it, could I?"

Jane shook her head slightly. "I've tried to take things for granted, the way other people do. To act as if I had all the time in the world. But that isn't true, either. There must be a happy medium. If only I could figure out what it was."

"Are you going to lose it again? I could use some warning this time."

"No, I'm not losing it. I feel better, actually."

"Good. I'm not sure I could handle another adrenaline surge. It's hard on the skin." Colette held a tiny rubber skirt up to her hips. "You could say those things to your father now."

"He's not around to hear them, remember?"

Colette stepped into the skirt and began to yank it up. It was like putting on a very tight girdle. "So? If there's an afterlife, he'll hear you. If there isn't, you won't know it yet." She adjusted the rubber at her waist and looked back over her shoulder to see how it fit her rear. Apparently, it was *too* short; her expert hand tugged the hem down a fraction of an inch. "Why don't you write about it in a poem? I'm putting it into my movie."

Jane looked at her, surprised. "Did you feel this way, after your accident?"

"This way, what?"

"That you had to live every second as if it was your last. That you should tell people things now, in case you don't get the chance later."

"No. I felt like God had played a bad practical joke on me, and I was going to get him back by doing what I wanted from then on. That wasn't a bomb, though."

"Oh, you're putting *a bomb* in your movie," Jane clarified. She'd thought Colette meant a sense of urgency.

"It'll be great. I hadn't really thought much about second-unit, special-effects kind of stuff. People want that."

"They do?"

"Anyway." Colette had lost interest in the topic. She placed her hands on her concave stomach. "What am I going to do with all these great clothes?" She pulled the rubber miniskirt off and replaced it with a flowery swath of light cotton that came to her knees. "I look like I'm wearing curtains. But what the fuck. It'll be worth it. Let's go treat ourselves, for being alive. I know just the place."

Jane realized two things; that she'd been wrong to think life would be more manageable with a stiff upper lip; and that she was hungry, too. Ravenous, as a matter of fact.

. . .

"And have you a reservation?" the maître d' asked.

Jane began to shake her head. Colette poked her.

"I'm the fiancée of Lord Kirby-Kerr. I believe you've seen me here before, with Lady Kirby-Kerr."

"Of course. Right this way."

As they walked down the short corridor toward the dining room, Jane became aware of a discernible hush. It seemed to her very English; it was the quiet afforded by tradition, continuity, confidence. She'd heard it in the phrase *think of England*. She heard it again as she crossed the threshold of the simple-yet-luxurious dining room, a calm that enveloped the chattering voices and chiming of silver on porcelain.

"Veni, vidi, vici," Colette whispered. She assumed her grand-entrance posture and glided forward, and, as she knew they would, people looked; not in the way they might have in Los Angeles, where according to Colette heads swiveled at every new entrance to a restaurant, in hopes of spotting a star or a mogul; but by London standards she caused a stir, if only in the form of sideways glances and eyebrows mildly raised. She didn't have to wear her outrageous wardrobe to command attention. She only had to stand up straight and dare people not to notice.

"These are my new cohorts," Colette said out of the side of her mouth. "Classy, eh?"

Jane thought the people looked like polished stones, hard and shiny. They intimidated her. The room was dark now, except for the low light from chandeliers and sconces, and the candles on the tables. Night had fallen; the windows were black. The diners appeared to have been gathered on purpose, so clear a picture did they present of a type: rich, entitled, comfortable. They were surely chosen, even if they had chosen themselves. She wished they'd gone somewhere else.

She was considering whether to suggest it when Colette came to a dead stop. Jane nearly ran into her.

"Hey, isn't that . . ." Colette pointed ahead.

Jane raised up on her toes to see past Colette's shoulder. There, to her surprise, was Uncle Francis, looking dapper in a beige seersucker suit and an orange tie printed with animals. She was very happy to see him. She assessed that he was with someone, although he happened to be sitting alone at the table at that moment. The chair opposite him had been pushed back several inches and angled to the side, as if someone had leapt from it seconds earlier. A rumpled napkin covered the plate.

Sensing the attention focused on him, he turned in their direction. At first he looked as pleased as Jane felt; then a cloud of doubt passed through his eyes. But he sprang to his feet, reaching his arms out.

"Jane!"

She gave the maître d' a shrug and brushed past the intervening tables, too excited to be self-conscious. Francis kissed her on both cheeks, then pulled her close and gave her a real hug. "Jane. I wish you had a phone," he said into her ear.

He sounded strained, and she pulled back to look at him. But all she could see was his familiar, open face, and a fresh, careful shave.

"I can't believe you're here! Colette spotted you."

She stepped back to make room for Colette, who held out her hand.

"Hello again." Francis bowed his head slightly. His manners had taken on international touches.

"Hello to you. Small world." Colette beamed flirtatiously.

"So it is." Francis still seemed preoccupied, but he rose to the occasion. "Please. Sit down. For a drink at least."

"We don't want to intrude on your evening," Jane said.

"Speak for yourself. I'd love to. We didn't even get to talk last fall," Colette said. She turned to the maître d'. "Please hold our table."

"You won't be sitting with the gentlemen?" The maître d' looked perplexed.

"We'll let you know." Colette was imperious.

The maître d' looked at Francis, who nodded. Within seconds additional chairs had been produced and Jane and Colette were seated and ordering drinks. Francis opened his cigarette case, and Colette pressed her hands to her heart. "Real Marlboros! I haven't had any since the last time you brought them."

"I have two cartons for you," Francis said.

A waiter produced a flame.

"You're a godsend," Colette said. She blew smoke out her nose.

"You're welcome. Now listen, I should tell you—" he said, and then stopped. His gaze lifted, past Jane's head. Rather than looking around, Jane continued to watch his face; she was still surprised to see him, and concerned by his somber mood. Colette was quicker to catch the scent of drama. Her eyes followed Francis's gaze, and as she turned to the side, her jaw dropped open, her head snapped up, and she muttered, *bloody hell*. Finally, Jane turned around. Nigel.

Nigel—Lord Kirby-Kerr—was Francis's dinner partner;

no wonder the maître d' had seemed confused. Jane was as happy to see him as she had been to find Francis there moments earlier. She didn't wonder why Nigel was there. They could all be together; what else mattered?

Jane raised her hand and waved, but Nigel didn't rush. On the contrary, he looked as though he'd prefer to run in the opposite direction, but he came over and kissed them each and picked up his napkin. A man in uniform scurried behind his chair and Nigel accepted his help perfunctorily. He belongs here, Jane thought. He isn't out of place.

"Hello, hello." He draped one arm over the back of his chair and gripped the lip of the table with his other hand.

"I thought you were going to see a friend tonight," Colette said.

"And I thought you were going to a film."

"We were at Hyde Park today when a bomb went off," she said crisply. "We're treating ourselves tonight. For being alive."

"I heard about that. Are you all right?" Francis reached across the table for Jane's hand.

"Don't we look it?" Colette widened her eyes.

"It was frightening," Jane said. "We weren't that close, although it felt as though we were at the time. I really hope no one was hurt."

Colette rolled her eyes, then looked around sharply. "So what is going on here, may I ask?"

The men exchanged glances. Francis seemed miserable; Nigel looked his usual handsome self. He picked up his Scotch and drained it.

"We met, as you know, in October," Francis said. He touched his silver nervously. Jane saw age in his face.

"When I sent you to the party," Jane added. She wanted to be of help.

"Yes. And then we stayed in touch."

Colette turned to Nigel. "You never mentioned it."

"No."

"You could have told me."

He avoided her eyes.

"Wasn't Francis helping you find a job?" Jane asked. She felt like Nonny, smoothing things over.

"Yes. And I believe I've found one."

Colette stared at him.

"In New York," he said. Finally, he looked at her.

"New York."

"You know I've always wanted to live in America."

Colette's ash fell. Absentmindedly, she rubbed it into the tablecloth. She stubbed the cigarette into the butter dish instead of the ashtray. Francis and Jane exchanged glances, but didn't stop her.

"It's in a decorating firm."

"And your writing?" Colette asked. "And your parents?"

"I haven't written anything in months. I wasn't any good, you know. I finally realized it, with Jane's help."

Jane was shocked. "I didn't mean you should stop." She glanced sideways at Colette, whose jaw was tight.

He shrugged. "As for my parents—I'm tired of my parents. Let my brother have everything. He'll allow me to visit, which will probably be as much as I'm going to want of the country anyway. I don't want to run the fairs and attend the weddings. It's not my life."

But all that money, Jane thought. Or had she heard Colette's thoughts? She wasn't sure whose side she was on. She didn't want there to be sides.

"I'm going to pay you back, Colette. I promise you that," Nigel said.

"Pay me back? How much? A year and a half of my life? What's that worth? Were you going to tell me, before you left?" Colette's voice had risen enough that people were watching. Jane had never seen her as upset. Where was her arsenal? Why wasn't she trying to persuade him?

"Let's not have a scene, shall we?" Nigel said. He picked at undiscernible specks on his pants.

Colette began to tremble.

"Let's take a walk, Jane," Francis said.

"Do you love him?" Colette demanded.

Jane heard Francis's suggestion, but she didn't move.

"Yes," Nigel said. "I love him. Why else? It would be smarter for me to marry you. You had a good idea, Colette. But that's what it is—an idea. Not a life."

"Jane," Francis prompted.

"It's all right," Colette told him. "I'll be the one to leave."

She strode past the chattering tables, unconcerned about making a scene. Jane stood up abruptly, too.

"Jane," Francis said, "we were going to tell you both."

"You should have."

"Please stay, Jane. This has nothing to do with you," Nigel said.

Jane saw he believed it. In his mind, their connection went just so far. It had only been she who believed it was all for one, one for all. She turned around. The room was a blur. She began to walk, feeling her way with her toes. She did not attract the level of interest that Colette did. She didn't care about maintaining her pride. She crept along, her heart pounding.

"Let her go," she heard Nigel say.

Francis did.

. . .

Colette was halfway down the block, walking fast. Jane had to run to catch up with her.

"Wait," Jane said. "Let's talk."

Colette glared at her, then walked even faster.

"Please, wait. We can straighten things out."

"Nigel's in love with your uncle. Nigel is moving to New York. How can talking straighten that out?"

"I don't know. We could make plans."

"Plans? These were my plans."

Their heels crunched on the sidewalk. The neighborhood was very quiet. If people were listening at their spring-wide windows, their interest in the spectacle on the street below was undetectable.

"I know," Jane said. "But there was always the chance of this happening, wasn't there?"

"By 'this,' do you mean your uncle?"

"I had nothing to do with this and you know it."

Colette stopped. Jane faced her.

"You had everything to do with this, Jane. You and your ideas about true love. You corrupted him!"

Jane might have laughed if she weren't so hurt.

"Colette, please. Let's get something to eat. I'm starving. You must be, too."

"How can you think about food at a time like this? You're really heartless, Jane."

"I'm going to pretend you didn't say that."

"Good plan. Keep on pretending. See if it gets you as far as it got me."

Colette stepped into the street and hailed a cab. When one stopped, she opened the door and stood back. "Get in."

Jane slid across the seat, but Colette didn't follow her. The door slammed shut.

"Where to?" the driver asked.

Quickly, Jane rolled down the window. "Are you all right?" she called out.

Without turning around, Colette raised her middle finger. Jane watched until the car reached the corner.

"Which way, Miss?"

"Highbury."

"Right!" He was clearly happy for the long, expensive ride across the city. "American, are you?"

When Jane didn't answer, he glanced in the rearview mirror. What he saw made him give up on conversation. He turned on the radio. *My aim is true*, claimed Elvis Costello.

"No music, please," Jane said, and closed her eyes.

. . .

She stood at the railing in front of the house, looking down at the picture window, watching him. He was at his desk, at work. He wore a black tee shirt that showed the muscles in his arms—lean, tight muscles. He didn't look like a writer. He looked like a carpenter.

She knocked on the window and let herself in.

"Can we talk?"

"I'm in the middle of something here," he said. He wasn't unfriendly; it was fact.

"I was in the middle of a bombing." She felt this was cheap, but she needed his attention.

"You were there? I saw it on the news."

"Colette and I were walking in the park." She began to shake. It was her longing, but he thought it was shock. Reluctantly, he took his fingers off the typewriter keys.

"Here, come sit for a moment."

He pulled her into his lap. Gratefully, she leaned against his chest.

"I'm fine. I was far away enough. And we knew that you and Nigel were in class, and safe."

"You were half right. I was there. Nigel hasn't been to class in weeks."

"So I found out. Why didn't you tell me he'd stopped coming?"

"It never came up. It's no big deal. He'll write or he won't, with me or without me."

"I told him his story was flat."

"So did I. So what?"

"Colette thinks it's my fault."

"She'll get over it."

Jane wasn't so sure. But she hadn't come to talk about Colette.

"I remembered things. Things I believe in. Things we haven't talked about. Things I want to talk about now."

"Uh-oh. This isn't going to be a life-is-precious-and-fleeting speech, is it? You know that isn't my territory. In my opinion life is cheap and long."

She'd so wanted for his contrarian positions to be right. If they were, she could always find a way to avoid being vulnerable. She picked up one of his big hands and matched hers to it.

"I wish that were true," she said, "but it isn't. Life is precious, and it's short. I know it. I've been pretending otherwise, and that's been a mistake. I'm not going to pretend anymore. I'm going to act on what I believe, instead of being amused by what you say you believe."

He flipped her wrist back and forth. He frowned. "Hey, are you hungry? You could go get some food while I do a little more work."

"I love you, Clay."

"Come on, Jane."

He put his hand over his face and groaned, and then revealed himself again, grinning; a bullying grin. She'd never called it that before, but it seemed clear, suddenly. How many of those had there been that she hadn't noticed?

She removed her hand from his and stood up. "I love you," she said. "How do you feel about me?"

He looked up at her, trying to find an angle on the situation. For once, she could see him thinking; this was not his area, and his thoughts were slow. He bent to the side for a pencil and tapped it impatiently on the edge of the table. When he hit on something, his eyes narrowed. "It's the letter, isn't it? You saw the letter and you're jealous."

She glanced over at the table. There was a letter from Sally West next to the typewriter. Instinctively, she glanced at the paper under the platen and saw he was writing her back. "Should I be jealous?"

"No. I've told you that. I don't believe in jealousy. Look, do you want to read it? You can, you know. I don't care."

"Full disclosure is the best hiding place," she said.

He cocked his head; she'd surprised him.

"You told me that, the first time we met."

That made more sense to him. He knew she wouldn't have thought that. "I have nothing to hide," he said. "Really. Read it if you'd like. I've never lied to you."

He picked it up and held it out to her. She remained still.

"If you must know, it's my divorce papers." He pulled them out of the envelope and waved them at her. "I told you I was getting divorced."

"I believed you."

"So what's the problem, then?"

She heard the people upstairs moving around, their footsteps clomping in a peaceful syncopation.

"Do I make you happy?" she asked.

His shoulders stiffened. He wasn't trying to jolly her anymore. "What?"

"Do I make you happy? It's a simple question."

"Jane, what's gotten into you?"

"I want to make you happy. I want you to feel happiness, and to call it happiness, and to believe in it. I want to have a family, a happy family. I've wanted it since I was born, and I always will want it, no matter what else I do. I want to be as close to someone as if he were my twin. To be completely on his side, and he on mine. To say anything."

"You can. I'm the last person who'd stop you."

She was about to argue, but she saw he meant this, and that he felt misrepresented. And, she realized, he was right. He'd never stopped her. He'd listed his beliefs and his rules, and she'd bent around them.

"I've stopped myself," she said, quietly, thinking it through as she spoke. "Because I was afraid to hear you say you believed we were different."

"I don't want children."

"Of course you don't. No eight-year-old wants children."

He gave a spontaneous, big laugh. The sound caught at her, like reaching arms. There was still a chance.

"Do you love me?" she asked.

"Jane, Jane, Jane. You know how I feel about that."

It was hard not to go along. How easy it would be to crawl into his bed and have him once again explain to her, in the cosseting dark, his ornery philosophy.

"Yes. I do. I just forgot for a moment. You know the effect a bomb can have on a person."

He thought she was giving up. Under those circumstances he could afford an embrace and he gave her one. "It's enough to make me a pacifist. I don't know if I could take too much of this." He tried to kiss her, but she wouldn't raise her mouth. The kiss landed in her hair. He pressed her head to his stomach. "Hear that growling? Do you think you could run out and pick us up some fish and chips? I had an idea this afternoon and I want to get it down before I forget it."

She picked up her bag. He sat down at his desk. He looked at home here; like her, he inhabited the room of a serious person, although Clay's seriousness was a vocation whereas hers was conditional. She thought she could give it up, under the right circumstances. He would never ask her to. She would always want him to ask.

"Could you pick up a few beers, too?"

He turned back to the job at hand, the letter to his only wife.

She stopped at the door. "How long before you finish your book?" she asked.

He held up his hand for silence. She closed the door behind her quietly.

. . .

On Wednesday night Jane went to Francis's hotel at the appointed time. If he'd been one of the knocks on the door in the past two days, she didn't know it. She hadn't answered the door, nor had she looked out the window to see who was walking away. She remained resolutely alone, packing and using the cleaning products the landlord had given her the first day. She'd bought six canisters of cleanser since then, but loyally stuck to his brand.

She called Francis from the house telephone in the lobby. He invited her up.

"I'd like to talk to you alone," she said.

There was a pause. She heard him place his hand over the mouthpiece.

"I'll come down," Francis said.

A few minutes later he appeared and guided her to the dark, elegant bar, his hand at her back. The room was full of couples who looked like them, successful older men with gleaming younger woman. A year ago she might have thought the other girls were there with their uncles, too, but now she knew better.

"I'm leaving tomorrow," Jane said after they'd ordered. She was sticking to ginger ale.

Francis took the news with stoicism. She was grateful he didn't try to change her mind. "Where will you go?"

"New York. It's time I get a job."

"Will we see you?"

The *we* hung between them. Jane tucked her hands under her thighs.

"Someday."

"What about Clay?"

Jane knew he'd ask that. She'd prepared for it. He didn't know much about it anyway. Whatever Nigel had told him.

She hadn't mentioned Clay often in her letters. Even there, she'd followed Clay's rules.

"We want different things," she said.

"I haven't been a very good godfather, have I?"

"I didn't marry a prince, as you hoped I would."

The couple at the next table had sidled close and were nuzzling each other. "I thought the English were supposed to practice decorum," she snapped.

Francis accepted her anger. "I think it's all about timing. In another era, Nigel wouldn't have had any choice about getting married, or working. Nineteen-eighty just happens to be an excellent time to be gay. You'll come with me to Fire Island. You'll see. That kind of freedom is worth the sacrifice of an estate in Sussex."

He spoke wistfully, and Jane realized how difficult his life must have been. How brave it was to declare his sexuality in the fifties, when boys like him were dating and marrying and lying. She supposed he'd earned an episode of subterfuge.

"So it's Nigel's freedom that interests you?" she teased.

"Freedom first. Then maybe a few other things." He picked up his glass and rattled the ice cubes.

"I'm glad you believe in love," she said.

"It does make for good days. If only that were enough."

"If only." Jane picked up her bag. "Go back to your good day." She leaned over to kiss him, Colette style, on both cheeks.

"You, too." They stood. "Are you going to see your mother?"

"I'm sure I will." Jane missed Via. But that had always been true.

"You're like her, you know."

"Via says I'm Emlin."

"People don't always see themselves clearly. Except us, of course."

"Of course."

They walked out of the bar holding hands. In the lobby the concierge discreetly averted his eyes. They were the picture of an affair all the way to the elevator.

"Well," Jane said.

Francis spread his arms. "Come here, you." He enveloped her in one of his big bear hugs. She allowed herself to lean against him, and breathed the scent of his aftershave and his suit. "It's out there for you, too, Jane. Don't give up."

"Even if I wanted to, I don't think I can."

He rubbed her cheek with his thumb, then stepped into the elevator.

"Say hi to Nigel for me. Although not too warmly."

He raised his hand. The doors shut.

Outside, it was still light in the sky, though the ground was dappled and shadowed. As she descended the steps of the Grosvenor House hotel, she looked across the street toward Hyde Park. The tree branches lifted in the breeze, showing the pale undersides of the leaves. It was a very beautiful evening. She headed up Park Lane and tried to memorize everything; she didn't know when she'd be back again. The gray buildings, so well suited to the frequent rain, seemed formal and slightly awkward in the spring breeze. She was glad she'd seen Francis, and felt the calm dignity of a person who's behaved according to her own heart.

Over the past few days, she'd come to understand why Via and Francis had always resented it so much when Nonny told them to *think of England*. They felt they were being directed to put their emotions aside. For Jane that was the very thing she wanted to do. She'd lost her father when she was too young to be able to bear it. She'd fled from that loss ever since, even across an ocean. Yet it was part of her; nothing could change that. Emlin had appeared to her in the Tower to remind her who she was. If she'd understood that then, she might not have made Colette, Clay and Nigel into mother, father, brother. She might have married a prince. Or found a soul mate.

She looked up at Marble Arch, half hoping to see the ghost again. There was nothing there, though, except the old city in the soft spring night.

She went down into the tube. She had one more stop to make.

. . .

She let herself in—the door wasn't locked—and instantly saw that the house wasn't itself; at least, it wasn't the way Nigel kept it. Ashtrays, and plates and glasses that had been used as ashtrays, sat on every surface. Clothes were dropped on the floor, as if Colette had undressed the moment she walked in. Jane walked from room to room. The kitchen was neat; Colette hadn't been eating. In the living room Nigel's careful alignments of candlesticks and vases and objets d'art had been undone, not, it seemed, maliciously, but out of simple lack of interest. Just Colette, moving around. Jane called her name.

"Go away." A voice from upstairs. Jane thought of the first time she'd come to the house, when Colette had been so happy to see her.

Jane trudged up. She stepped into Colette's room but found it empty. "Where are you?"

"Hell. Bloody hell, as it were."

Jane followed the voice down the hall to Nigel's room. She stepped on the glossy floor—Nigel had applied coat after coat of polyurethane—and saw at once that the room was in the opposite condition of the rest of the house. The surfaces were empty of all his personal effects. His stack of sketches was gone. The furniture stood in place, but he couldn't very well cart that to Grosvenor House. The space had become just a space. For the first time, Jane missed him.

Colette was sitting primly on the bench, her knees and feet pressed together. She wore only her bra and underpants. The new hair she'd grown to be a peeress had all been chopped off and she wore no makeup, so she had only her bare girl's face to contort. It didn't hide much.

She looked up at Jane. Her eyes were small without their armor of shadow and mascara. Small and sweet, with short lashes like a cat. "What was he doing in here all that time, if he wasn't writing?" she asked in bewilderment.

Jane glanced at the exquisitely painted walls. "I want you

to come to New York with me. I'm leaving tomorrow." Jane ached to describe the whole bad night she'd had after they last parted, but she hadn't come to talk about herself. There'd be plenty of time for that—she hoped. "I ended it with Clay."

Colette nodded, nonplussed. She seemed dazed and passive. Jane recognized the condition. Grief.

"I'm going to get a job, and maybe go back to school. And you could finish your movie. I'll help you."

Colette gave her a bland smile. Jane wasn't reaching her. "How long have you been sitting here?" The room was hot and close. She opened a window to the night and was assailed by a metallic smell; rain coming.

"Not long." She touched her hips, front and back, where pockets would be. "I don't have my cigs."

"I'll get them for you."

Jane hurried back down the hall and found the pack on the night table. She was about to leave when she saw a white arm protruding from under the bed. She'd forgotten about the wedding dress. She kicked it back until it was no longer visible. On her way out she saw the old photograph she liked so much under a pile of scarves. She carried it, too, back to Nigel's room.

Colette lit up.

"So what do you think? Will you come?" She handed Colette the picture. "You could be her again."

Colette straightened a creased corner. "No, I wouldn't. This girl was innocent." She looked around for where to flick her ash. Jane glanced around the room, but there was nothing. She sat down next to Colette and handed over her shoe.

"Use this."

Colette stared at it, then tapped gray cinders onto the floor. Even Nigel's perfect room wasn't sacred anymore.

"You'll meet someone else," Jane said. "There are men in New York who'd adore you. Dozens. With tons of money."

Colette leapt up. The picture sailed to the floor. "Like who? Who, Jane? No man is ever going to adore me. You've seen me!"

For a moment Jane honestly didn't understand that Colette was referring to her scars. Then she remembered when she first saw her hands.

"Colette, you're the most beautiful woman I've ever seen. No one even notices after a little while."

"But who's going to bother getting past that little while?"

"Lots of people. Anyone worth knowing." She retrieved the photograph and looked at the hopeful girl. "You're not the only one with scars, you know."

Colette sat back down and slumped forward, one arm across both knees, the other propping up her head. Church bells rang nearby, and a car cut its engine on the street.

"It didn't matter to Nigel, of course."

"Is that why you picked him?"

"No."

"Then why? I don't believe it was only the money."

Jane had begun to comprehend the truth, but she wanted to hear it from Colette. She wanted some honesty at the end of the day.

Colette crossed her legs. "You asked if I ever felt about anybody the way you do about Clay."

"Oh, Colette. Why didn't you tell me?"

"What would you have said?"

Jane didn't answer.

"See?" Colette said.

Jane nodded. "We've done well. A gay man for you, a man on the rebound for me."

"It could be worse."

"How?"

"Ax murderers." She poked at her scalp. "I have to do my hair. I'm thinking blue this time."

Jane sighed. "I feel so much older than I did a week ago."

"It's about time. So when are you leaving?" Colette asked. She lit a fresh cig.

Jane knew she'd said, but she repeated the information.

"That's too soon. I couldn't possibly come tomorrow. Maybe in a couple of weeks."

"I'll write as soon as I have an address."

"Okay. Hey, would you mind letting yourself out? I was about to take a bath."

"I love you, Colette," Jane said.

"Oh, Jane. I love you, too. But what good does that do us? You have to stop thinking that love is going to change your life."

Jane tried to embrace her, but Colette remained stiff and unyielding. "Go," she said.

Jane walked back down the hall, down the heavy staircase

and, for the last time, out the curtained glass door. Before shutting it, she pressed the button that flipped the latch, so it would lock behind her. She did not look back.

. . .

The next morning Jane was packed and ready early, her suitcases by the door. She felt utterly alone. Not even the mouse was there, skittering across the counter to keep her company. She'd stuffed cheese in the wall and then plugged up the hole, fearing the next tenant might not find him as companionable. No trace of either of them remained.

She sat at the table to watch for the car. A light rain fell out of a white, glaring sky, filling the air with moisture that seeped into the flat.

The mailman rounded the walk and bounded up the steps. He wore his uniform shorts and held an umbrella over his head. She'd written him a note with her forwarding address. She'd planned to leave it on her way out, but here he was.

"Back to America then, Miss?"

Jane nodded. He looked at the note.

"New York, is it. Be careful there. It's thick with muggers."

"I'll be careful."

"You don't have to worry in London, Miss."

Not unless you mind bombs and razor slashings and murders and marauding football fans and drunks pouring out the pubs every night at eleven.

"No, it's nice here," Jane said.

"Here's two letters before you go. Lucky you caught me."

She took the letters back upstairs. It was difficult to decide which one to leave for last. She ran an index finger lightly across the markings on the envelope that formed her name in handwriting. He'd pressed hard in writing them. He held his pen wrong, above the second joints of his thumb and middle finger; hadn't his mother helped him? She'd probably tried. Jane took a breath, and opened the envelope from The *New Yorker*.

Dear Ms. MacLeod,

These are too coded for us, but they show a good ear.
Try us again.

She thought of her literal poems. Didn't people recognize love when they saw it anymore? She laid the page on her lap and opened Clay's. It was a page of onionskin paper covered with red typing.

Jane.

I do not think you should assume that I will become happy due to your efforts, or that you should want me to make such an effort on your behalf. In fact, I do not think you should even want me to be happy. What both of us ought to be, I think, are makers of lives with thoughts and feelings and deeds that create an existence that is of value. I think we should be right before we are happy. If happiness is feeling good, then it is too expensive when the cost is that it displaces good ideas.

Will I make you dinner every night when you have the flu? Will I hold you and let you cry when you do not want to explain but just want to cry? Will I always be kind to you? Will I promise that I will watch you get old and not so great-looking and help you die? Will I have children with you, and do all those things for them, perform those mindless custodial duties?

This is the contract you want from me, and I can't agree to it. Not out of hand. I would like to think I'll be able to fulfill some of these auxiliary needs of yours, but I'm not sure that will happen. I am sure it's not what's important.

Don't you see that to do those things increases the possibility of darkening another world? Whoever can do those things cannot simultaneously fill another, more subtle universe of personality. If you make dinner every night for someone with the flu there is much you have done but there is much else you have not done and most likely cannot do. It is a kind of support we seek from others, this rudimentary caretaking, but you should not imagine that because it is easy to desire and the desire is clear (since we all do desire it) that you or anyone can ask for this manner of support and expect it will be provided in addition to other kinds of support that secure us. There is support, too, that demonstrates that you are extraordinary and makes way for you to become a part of surprising things. If you seek people who give strength day-to-day against the ordinary, then you will not be able to recognize people who can give you strength to find the extraordinary.

This is what we should be for each other . . .

I fear that it will be your habit to hang on to notions of what you want that seem right because they are familiar when it never was familiarity that was at stake. Tenderness has never been at stake. The issue is not pain or caring or happiness. What is smart, what is not, this is at stake. Mind is at stake. Thinking is. Feeling warm on the skin when the day is cold is agreeable. But it is not of true value except to people who have lost the capacity to be serious and to generate value.

Tell me that you do not want anyone to correct you and I will tell you that you are lying. If you go where there are no demands, you may find that next time you are asked, you will have nothing to give.

I hope you appreciate that gentleness is often apparent when there is nothing in the head.

I wish that you remain unsatisfied, and that you don't come upon happiness too easily.

I wish this for you more than I've ever hoped this for anyone. You see? Which is why I'll never say I love you, because it couldn't ever mean enough.

Clayton

She read it twice in a row, taking care to remain open-minded and receptive even as her nerves chimed. Clay was challenging her to be extraordinary. He was offering her an exalted life, beyond everyone else's rules. He believed they could be the exception. They didn't need families or security.

They didn't even need to say the things that other people did. It was a sublime vocation to which he was calling her. A once-in-a-lifetime chance.

The car horn bleeped below. She held both letters in her hands.

"Bullshit," she said aloud, and ripped them in half.

2000

THERE WAS NOTHING LEFT Jane could do to stall. The overnight bag she'd packed for herself and Emily sat by the front door. She'd brushed Marmalade, cleaned his cat box, and put down enough food to last him until the next afternoon, and she'd checked that the gates that opened onto the fire escape were locked. There'd been less crime in Manhattan recently, but it was foolish to take chances.

"Ready, Em?"

Emily was sitting on the sofa in the living room. She looked up from her book. "I've been ready for three hours."

She was eager. Unaffected by Jane's dread, which Jane had done her best to hide.

"I know. I'm ready now, too. I told Via we'd be there by four."

Emily went to the mirror. She became pensive and critical when she looked at herself, and portrayed none of her bright gameness. Jane supposed she was trying to look older.

Emily began to twist her shoulders to the side, but when she glanced up and noticed Jane watching, she quickly pulled

the front strands of hair behind her ears and raised her eyebrows in a self-mocking, resigned way. At nine she'd become
self-conscious.

"You look very pretty," Jane said.

"Are we really going to sleep in a tent?" She came over to
Jane and wrapped her thin arms around Jane's waist. Her
head stopped just short of Jane's clavicle.

"Apparently so. The weather is supposed to be perfect."
Jane felt an anxious pinch in her stomach. "Hey, would you
call Uncle Francis and tell him we'll be there in twenty minutes?"

"Sure."

Jane walked to the doorway of her bedroom and looked
around, as if half hoping to be confronted with a disaster that
would require her immediate attention. But the room was as
pristine as always; she had a double bed made with a white
blanket cover, a small bookshelf, a reading lamp, and a bench
on which sat neat piles of books, magazines, bills. All her
clothes were in the closet; her sparse wardrobe consisted
mostly of black pants and navy shirts that she replaced when
they wore out. The room was her nun's cell, a minimally
adorned space suited to a solitary, focused life. Jane wasn't
particularly religious, but she had a faith; she was devoted to
insuring Emily a happy childhood. If that meant Jane had to
endure time with her family, so be it. She was the adult; she
could wear the poker face.

She was about to close the door when she impulsively
grabbed a book and put it in her shoulder bag.

"All set?" she called.

"Yup."

They met up by the kitchen.

"Uncle Francis says he'll be in the lobby."

This is for her, Jane thought. "Great. Let's go."

. . .

Francis and Nigel lived in a doorman building on Central Park West. Every Thanksgiving they left town for the weekend but opened the apartment to friends so their children could watch the parade up close; the heads of the enormous balloon characters stared directly in the windows, frightening the smaller children to tears. Francis was against the parade and its sponsor. He prided himself on the fact that never once, in all the years he'd lived in New York, had he set foot in Macy's. Nigel informed him that Macy's had become a proper New York institution, and that there were far better targets for his snobbery, but Francis wouldn't hear of it: Macy's was the nadir. Jane said it placed him that he could afford to believe that. Francis happily agreed.

When Jane and Emily arrived at Francis's building, they found Nigel sitting in the car.

"Are you coming?" Emily asked. She loved Nigel. He often took her to FAO Schwarz and told her to pick out anything she wanted.

He got out but left the engine idling. "No, no. I just pulled the car around. That's as far as I go in the direction of a family reunion. Lucky me," he said, looking at Jane.

She accepted his empathy. He knew how she felt. "So what are you going to do this weekend?"

"Work. Sketches for a townhouse in the Village owned by a twenty-six-year-old movie star."

"Who?" Emily asked.

He leaned down to whisper in her ear.

Emily jumped, pulling her heels straight up to her fanny. It was the confined, efficient expression of a city child's glee, energy expended upward when there was no room to run.

"Can I meet her?"

"Of course. I wrote it into my contract."

Jane saw a passerby stare at him. His hair still slipped boyishly over his forehead. He noticed the glance, too, but paid it no real attention. Instead he watched Francis emerge briskly from the revolving door. The bemused, knowing look on Nigel's face wasn't one Jane could watch for long without feeling as though she was intruding on an intimacy; yet the exchange was too compelling for her to ignore. Francis returned Nigel's look with his own version, one that referred to twenty years of private jokes. Then, the connection having been made, they broke it and reverted to their characteristic polite formality. Francis kissed her on both cheeks.

"Would you mind driving?" he asked.

"Not at all."

Nigel handed her the keys.

"Don't do anything I'd do," Francis said to him.

"Back at you." Nigel loved American expressions. He and Emily waved at each other until Jane turned the corner.

"Are you going to miss him, Uncle Francis?" Emily asked.

Francis reached his arm over the back seat and she took his hand. "Oh yes. It's your job to cheer me up."

"I'll try," she said.

Francis laughed. "I'm joking, Em." He shook his head and looked at Jane.

"Don't say it," she told him, for she knew what he was thinking—*she's so much like you.*

Jane didn't like hearing that, though logically it was hard to refute. Emily had no father beyond the basic biological material. When Jane turned thirty-five with no husband in sight, she'd gone to a sperm bank. On the first try she'd conceived twins, one of whom, a male fetus, had stopped developing halfway through the gestation period. Emily, however, was healthy and vivid—and she did resemble Jane with her green eyes, fuzzy hairline, and desire for serenity. There were traits of hers, though, that Jane didn't like seeing passed along. Emily's seriousness, for example. Her watchfulness. Jane tried to indulge her, even to spoil her, but rather than developing a sense of entitlement, Emily became more thoughtful and responsible. On those trips to FAO Schwarz with Nigel, she never asked for much—exactly what Jane would have done when she was a child.

How did Emily's genetic father reveal himself? Emily had a lovely mouth, and a dimple in one cheek. She could sing.

. . .

The occasion for the gathering was Via's sixty-fifth birthday. Ned Phelps had sent invitations to all Via's children and their families to spend the night in tents on the property. It was the first time they'd all get together since Nonny's and Grand's funerals, which had both occurred during the same year when Emily was two. Emily had never seen them as a group; Jane had declined to tell her that there were good reasons why. Jane had observed that many families who experienced a trauma pulled closer, but there were those that never fully recovered, hers among them. They were the only family Emily had, however, so Jane had always portrayed them as only circumstantially separated. It was a charade, but not a harmful one. It put Jane in the odd position, however, of creating as a fiction the sort of tight, jolly family for which she used to long.

.   .   .

"Read anything interesting lately?" Francis asked.

She glanced over. He looked down at her bag, then back up at her. She'd been caught.

"I don't know why I brought it," she said. "I grabbed it at the last minute."

"May I have a look?"

She nodded. He pulled the book from her bag.

"'*Letters of Explanation*, by Clayton West,'" he read. "Good title. How is it?"

Jane glanced in the rearview mirror. Emily had her headphones on.

"Pretty good." She felt queasy discussing it, even with Francis. She knew a woman who spoke about a well-known actor she'd gone out with in college as if they were in daily contact, which always struck her as pathetic and absurd. From how far off could glory reflect? Clay was a very distant sun. Only once or twice had she claimed that his light had ever reached her. Unfortunately, one of those moments of weakness had occurred at work, where a mention of a connection to an author was least likely to be forgotten. She was an editor in the Museum of Modern Art's publications department. Everyone around her was an avid reader.

She still cringed when she thought of it. Her boss had said he thought Clay was up there with Thomas Pynchon and Hemingway. She responded by saying she used to be his girlfriend. Not a proud moment.

"Are you ever in contact with him?" Francis asked.

"No. I'm still on his gratis list, though. I always receive his books."

"No note?"

"Nope." She wished he'd take a hint from her monosyllabic answers and drop the subject. But Francis liked to discuss he said/she said matters as thoroughly as any teenage girl.

"So what's it about?"

She was afraid he was going to ask that. "A man writes a letter asking for an explanation of what everyone who's disappeared from his life has been doing since the last time he saw them. He asks them to say, also, if their life has been better without him. He gives as a return address a motel in the California desert, where he sits and waits for the replies."

"Does he get any?"

"Quite a few."

"Is their life better without him?"

He opened the cover and began to turn the pages.

"Some say so . . ." In her mind she began to beg, please, please, forget it now, don't see it, close the book—

He found it.

"For J.?"

She shrugged.

"He dedicated the book to you and all you can do is shrug?"

"It's not me. We haven't spoken in twenty years. How many J.'s do you think he knows by now? I know about fifty myself."

"Is he married?"

"No. I don't think so. What's your point?"

"I can tell you haven't thought about this."

She made a fist and socked him.

"Ouch! That hurt!" He rubbed his arm. "Touched a nerve, did I?"

"It's not me. Forget it, will you?"

He scowled as if she was being ridiculous. "Has your life been better without him?"

"It would be better without you, I know that much."

Her entire head was burning. She giggled, but not from a place of mirth. It was nerves, stretched and stretched again, as if her nervous system had been wound around one of those old saltwater-taffy machines at the shore.

"You're J., you're J." He poked his index fingers at her.

"What's going on?" Emily asked.

Jane glanced in the rearview. Em's brow was furrowed.

"Nothing. Uncle Francis is acting his shoe size rather than his age, that's all."

"He always does that," Em said, and pulled her headphones back over her ears.

"You always do that," Jane said.

"My European shoe size is forty-six, I'll have you know. And you're the one with your old boyfriend's book in your handbag."

When there was no room to maneuver, Jane was capable of having a sense of humor about herself. "You have a point. All right, I admit, it crossed my mind that maybe I'm J. But I sincerely doubt it, after all this time. And anyway, there's no way of knowing."

"You could ask," Francis said.

"I could become an astronaut," she said.

"I think asking if you're J. or not would require slightly less in the way of major life changes." He looked at her astutely. "Or would it?"

"I thought you were going to stop talking about it."

"I am. I'm going to read."

. . .

She'd found the package one day earlier that summer when she arrived home from work. It was downstairs in what passed for a lobby in her building, leaning up against the dirty, mustard-colored wall in what passed for a method of handling packages. She carried it upstairs and didn't think about it again until later that night after Emily left for an evening playdate with a friend. Emily had been invited to

spend the night, but as usual, she declined that part of the invitation; she wasn't ready for sleepovers. Jane had been
thinking about that, wondering about Emily's need to stay
close to her—had she imparted an insecurity?—when she casually ripped open the package and saw the author's name.
Oh. So he'd written another novel. She tried to remember
when the last one had come out, and couldn't readily do so,
so she supposed it was about time.

The cover showed a picture of an envelope, with swaths
of blue above and below. The address read *Letters of Explanation;* the return address, in the upper left-hand corner,
said, "Clayton West, The Mojave Desert, California." In
spite of the fact that she knew better, she looked for a dedication. There never was one in any of his books, which, the
first two times she'd observed it, when the hurt of their part-
ing was still present in her body, confirmed her perceptions
of his deficiencies: Solipsism. Arrogance. Misanthropy. Yet
as decades passed, and none of it mattered to her anymore—
her relationship with him became a blink compared to the
infinity of Emily—she was able to smile again at his orneriness. But only for a moment. The fact was, she didn't care.

To her surprise, there was a dedication this time.

For J.

She flushed; was it possible? Forget it, she chided. It was
not she. Definitely not. Why would he contact her now, after
all this time, and in this way? They had nothing to say to
each other. It was such a long time ago. She continued to

name the reasons why it was impossible even as she pulled the manila envelope out of the trash and checked again for a note. Nothing. Naturally.

When Emily came home that night, she was still reading, and Jane hurried her to bed so she could finish. It was hard for her to even judge whether or not it was good. She couldn't stop herself from picturing Clay as the character he called Y who sat in the desert waiting for his return mail; and she read the replies half believing—more than half—they were from real people who'd known him. Some of them had clear ideas about whether or not they were better off without him, but most of them didn't know, an outcome she found both clever and disconcerting. She'd always assumed she was better off, but was that definite?

Since reading Clay's book, she'd walked around with the question he'd posed in her mind, and she'd thought of snatches of lines she might put in a reply. She never remembered them long enough to write them down, however— they were a parlor game. In the end, there was only one answer; if she were still with Clay, she wouldn't have Emily. That was the unthinkable.

JANE HAD A TENT to herself. Theoretically, she was to share it with Emily, but the early arrivals decided that all the cousins would sleep together in a big heap in the middle of the field. It was only five o'clock, but they'd already laid out their sleeping bags, and anyone tracking their movements would have noticed a pattern of trips to the kitchen and a stashing of supplies back at base camp. Jane was tracking them to some degree; she was a city mother, not used to turning her back. She couldn't imagine, however, what the children found worth taking from Via and Ned's kitchen; it had been a big event when they'd added raw almonds to their abstemious repertoire. Mary Beth, Sean's wife, had thought to bring brownies and lemonade. Perhaps Caroline, who lived nearby, had wisely stocked the pantry.

Via had nine grandchildren—or sixteen if you counted Ned's, too, but no one on either side lumped them all together. They ranged in age from twenty down to eight. Sean and Mary Beth had four girls, all with Scottish names: Elspeth, Kenna, Cait, and Greer. Alex and Karen had two boys, Carson and Blair; and Caroline and Paul had managed to reproduce in proper fifties style, a boy and a girl spaced two years apart, properly named William and Elizabeth—no nicknames, please. Grand's genes had dominated in Jane's generation, but in general the children resembled the in-laws more than the MacLeods, although Emily, like Jane, was said to look like Emlin.

From a slight, quiet little girl, Caroline had become a boisterous, clubby matron. She'd never lost weight after her second child, but she carried it well; she preened and streaked, and ended up looking quite sexy. She and her husband, an equally heavy, loud banker named Paul Neuberg, lived in Wynnemoor, where Caroline worked as a realtor. Paul's greatest frustration in life was that people tended to assume he was Jewish because of the sound of his last name, and he'd developed a habit of mentioning his pure German ancestry in every conversation. If Francis happened to be present when Paul made his shrill claim, he made the counterclaim that there was Jewish blood in Caroline's background, to which Paul responded with a belly laugh. He thought Francis was a panic.

Alex and Karen lived in Washington, where Alex was a lawyer and Karen a lobbyist for big agribusiness concerns; she switched too often for anyone to remember which one in particular. She was admirably efficient and attractive, but she took offense easily and, under the rubric of good manners, overthanked and overacknowledged Via for her generosities, to the point of rudeness. Alex thought she was terrific, though, so everyone tried to like her. "She's made the most of herself," Francis said slyly.

Sean was a television news director. He and Mary Beth lived in Tarrytown, New York, where she took care of the four girls, their pets, the house, and still managed to perform good deeds in the community. She was who Francis would have been if he'd been born a woman. Who Via had tried to be, Jane thought.

Jane was the last to arrive, but only by a few minutes. Caroline and Alex had come just before, approaching the driveway from opposite directions at the exact same moment. Everyone laughed about it; they'd been performing such twin tricks all their lives. Emily pulled on Jane's arm.

"They're twins?"

"You know that, Em."

"I guess I forgot."

That was the last time Jane had spoken with Emily. Seconds later she'd been swept up by the cousins. Her likeness to Jane showed again; she was as thrilled as Jane would have been at her age to run off laughing with her extended family.

Via was putting Francis up in the house, but everyone else was bivouacked in the tents. Ned had rented portable showers and flush toilets, which were secreted among the trees. Jane unpacked her bag, laying clothes and shoes along the edge of the drop cloth. She had the front flap of the tent open and kept turning to look at the framed view. For their twilight years, as Sean said to tease them, Ned and Via had bought a small gentleman's farm that happened to typify an English style of country comfort. Via had ended up thinking of England after all.

. . .

The schedule called for the adults to gather at six on the terrace for drinks. Via was there first; she couldn't both be the
main attraction and make an entrance; that would make her
too anxious. She only liked being the center of attention of
the person to whom she was married.

Jane was the first of the guests to appear. Also typical. Via
smiled at her. "You look nice."

"Thanks. So do you."

It always surprised Jane to see how old Via's face had become. She still seemed so vigorous, and the memory of her
as a young woman was far outweighed by the amount of
time Jane had spent with her as an adult. The only thing Via
did to disguise her age was to color her hair a brownish red,
and to wear it jauntily cut so that it framed her face and
feathered her neck. She wore an old silk Nehru jacket and a
pair of burnt-orange silk pants that Jane remembered from
their summers at Nonny and Grand's shore house. Via had
bought clothes since then, of course; but it was very like her
not to buy anything new to wear to a party given in her
honor. Though Via's motives had little to do with style, she
looked stylish. She had the eye to save the right clothes.

Via glanced around and began to move the furniture.

"Let me help you," Jane said.

"I want to move this sofa over there."

They picked up the wicker sofa. Nigel would have at least
enjoyed this portion of the program, Jane thought.

"That's better. Would you like a glass of wine?"

Via's head bobbed slightly. Jane realized she'd already

been drinking. The requisite dressing drink. She drank far less than she used to, but even the slightest amount affected her.

"No, thanks," Jane said. She couldn't enjoy it around Via.

"Well." Via poured herself a glass. "Alex brought this. It's very good."

Obligingly, Jane looked at the bottle. A Montrachet. "Wow."

"It's the kind of thing he spends money on."

They smiled.

"Emily seems well," Via said. "Is she going to eat anything tonight?"

Jane bristled. This was so Via. One hand giveth, the other taketh away. "She hardly ever gets sick."

"I don't understand how children eat these days. When you were little, I made dinner and you all ate it. That was that. Now everyone has to have a completely different meal. I wouldn't put up with it."

"Things have changed," Jane said. "Parents don't want to be authoritarian anymore. People remember what they didn't like about their childhoods and they try to offer their children better experiences."

Via set her glass on a table. She crossed her arms and hung her head.

"What?" Jane asked. Although she knew. She'd been hurt by Via's criticism of Emily, and had struck back. Immediately she regretted it. "Mom, I didn't mean—"

"Didn't mean what?" Sean bopped up the steps.

"Never mind," Via said. She picked up her drink again and

relaxed. Sean never upset her. "We were just setting things up. Would you like some of Alex's wine?"

Sean rubbed his hands and walked to the drinks table. "Alex springs," he said, examining the bottle.

Jane considered leaving.

"Delicious," Sean said.

If it were only herself, she'd get in the car and go. She was forty-five years old. She didn't need this.

"Are any of your friends coming? Aunt Gay, or Aunt Susan?" Sean poured himself a glass. He looked very handsome with gray at the temples. He wore a wedding ring, and a second ring he and Mary Beth had bought to celebrate their twentieth anniversary.

"They'll be here soon, for drinks," Via said. "After that, it will be just us."

Jane looked out over the meadow where the younger children were playing tag. Emily was in the thick of it, her hair and arms flying in opposite directions. "Do you need me to do anything?" she asked. She could at least be busy.

"There's a platter of crudités on the kitchen table," Via said. "Thank you."

Jane began to walk toward the door before she even finished her sentence. As she passed through the hall, she noticed a row of cardboard boxes—odd that they hadn't been cleared away. She also saw furniture that had been Nonny's, and furniture from the Willow Lane house. Emily had a bed from Nonny's house, thick wood with carved pineapple finials. Over the years Jane had spotted other items in the dwellings of her siblings. It was only right that they should each have things that were their father's and their grandparents'; she knew that. She even believed it. Yet it still felt fundamentally awful to her that everything had been split up.

. . .

She dawdled in the kitchen talking to the energetic college kids who worked for the caterer and pretending she had a better idea for how to arrange the carrots and celery on the huge silver tray that Grand had received from his company for fifty years of service. By the time she returned to the terrace, the guests had arrived.

Her siblings were all there, of course. Her brothers both held themselves in the way men do who have achieved some degree of success; how long ago had they stopped appearing at parties with comb marks in their hair? Caroline had a sweater tied around her plump brown shoulders. She looked to see what Jane was carrying. "Crudités! How perfect!" She swiped a carrot through the onion dip, then took another before turning back to her conversation.

One of the college kids took the tray from Jane. She felt vulnerable as she watched it sail away. She'd wanted the armor.

Via had many friends, several of whom she'd known since she was married to Emlin. None of them were still married to the husbands they'd had then. Some of them were single, with money, and seemed very content. They did a lot of traveling, and asked Via to go with them, but she declined. She was attached to Ned and grew anxious when they were separated, even for a day or two. She couldn't understand the lives of single women, but Jane looked to them for inspiration.

She approached Aunt Gay. Like Via, the only thing that betrayed her age were the lines on her face. She was cheery and liberal-minded; she loved to spar with Ned about his gentleman-farmer's brand of conservative politics.

"I wish your grandparents could be here," she said. "They'd love to see all of you together. It was your grandfather's dream."

"It didn't exactly work out in a dreamy way, unfortunately," Jane said. "Remember what happened at Grand's funeral." There'd been arguments and accusations. A dinner at a restaurant was a fiasco, with Caroline walking out and Alex getting drunk and saying the kinds of things against Grand that Via liked to hear. Not to mention the competition over who would get what from the house.

"That was bad," Gay agreed. "But Via's children are very loyal to her. I know a lot of people who don't have that."

"We don't have a choice," Jane laughed.

Gay didn't laugh with her. "Your father would be proud of you all."

"Was this his dream, too?" Jane asked.

"No, no, I don't think so. I think his dream was Via," Gay said.

"Via?"

"Yes. He changed his whole life for her, you know. He once told me that before he met Via he imagined having a small practice in a rural place, or that he'd go to Asia or India and train doctors there. But she wanted to stay in Wynne-moor."

"She hated Wynnemoor. She hated living near her parents."

Gay looked at her. "How could she live without that?"

Jane was astonished. "You mean she didn't want to get away from them?"

Gay shook her head. "Jane, Jane, Jane. You were always so earnest. It must have been impossible for you to understand someone who had no instinct for growing up."

.   .   .

When she thought about it, which she didn't much anymore, it surprised Jane that she hadn't gotten married. She'd certainly intended to; if not literally married, she'd believed she'd find a partner with whom she could share her life and thoughts. She'd never imagined she'd be without such a person by her age. She'd been busy, though, since Emily was born. She tried to go out for a while when Em was a baby, but it had been too hard. She had a couple of bad baby-sitter experiences and that was that. Anyway, it seemed nonsensical to leave Emily alone with strangers when Jane had wanted her so much. There was no blind date she'd like better than she liked her child, she was sure of that. And she'd had her fun. She'd been in love; for a few months in London, before the boundaries and limitations began to show, she'd had a mate in Clay. When she needed transport, she still thought of England, but it had become a memory rather than a promise. That was all right. Emily's turn was coming up, and when that happened, Jane wanted to be there to help.

. . .

"Sshh!"

The mothers turned around from the long table where the adults sat to the card tables behind them. The children had gone wild tapping forks against their glasses and couldn't bring themselves to stop.

Ned stood at the head of the table waiting to make a toast.

Jane sat between Paul and Alex, who talked sports across her. To preserve her equanimity, she was focused on the flowers in the centerpieces, all of them fresh from the garden.

"Okay, enough," Ned said. He held his hands shoulder height and pressed them down.

"Sshh. Emily!"

Jane started. Emily? She hadn't even turned around to calm her, because she knew she'd be the first to stop. But Emily was laughing, her cheeks filled with hectic color. She clanked her glass again.

"Enough," Jane said.

Mary Beth pulled the knife from Emily's hand. Emily giggled, pressing her hands against her face.

Jane gave her a look, and then wished she hadn't when Emily's face fell. She decided not to look around again no matter what she heard behind her.

"Well," Ned said. "I'm not going to say much, because you know how Via is."

Everyone laughed. They did.

"But I did want to offer an official toast on this the occasion of Via's *mmnn-mmnn*"—he mumbled the number into his hand, adhering to the tired conformity of shame about aging—"birthday. I've known her for thirty of those years, and they've certainly been the happiest of mine. So here's to many more."

He raised his glass. Jane heard the crack of the children's thick glasses behind her, but she paid no obvious attention.

Sean stood. He touched his hand to his chest, positioning a phantom tie. "I've been trying to think of what to say. How can you make a toast to your own mother in a reasonable amount of time? It would take me all night to name the ways that Via has influenced me, and to repeat all my memories. I can't do you justice, Mom. The most I can say is that I see a lot of you in my children, and that makes me very happy."

Everyone clapped.

Francis stood up. "I've always been Via's older brother. There came a time when I began to think of myself as her older sister. She never minded that. It's hard for me to describe how valuable that casual acceptance was to me. If it weren't for her, I may have turned out like Paul."

Caroline put her hand over her mouth. Paul grinned, however. He could afford to; what did Francis have on him? When Caroline saw that he wasn't upset, she began to laugh and flicked her wrist at Francis. "You should be so lucky!" she called out.

"Don't I know it," Francis said. "But I wasn't so lucky. I was what I was. Via allowed it, when no one else even wanted

to admit it existed. I am forever grateful to you, little sister."
He raised his glass. "Although I do think you could use a little Botox, and maybe some work along the jawline."

Groans. Jane could hear the younger children asking puzzled questions. *He's gay*, one of the teens explained; Sean's daughter Kenna, it sounded like.

Caroline stood. "Don't y'all get tired of the way men give the toasts and the women just sit there as if they've got nothing to say? I mean, isn't this the twenty-first century?"

Since when did she develop a Southern accent, Jane wondered?

"So I'm doing my part for the feminine sex. Mom, you're the greatest!"

Alex's Montrachet was holding up. Jane had succumbed during the meal, and was glad of it. It tasted of France.

Paul elbowed her. "Aren't you going to say something?"

It hadn't occurred to her. Via hated toasts. Who were they for, then? She didn't need to give a performance.

"Come on, Jane." Alex poked her from the other side.

She stood. All the faces, lit by candles, turned toward her. She was the oldest child. It was incumbent upon her to have the last word.

"To Mom," she said. "If you loved me as much as I love Emily, I must have been a very happy baby."

Everyone looked at her expectantly, not quite understanding. She didn't understand herself. What could she say?

"Cheers," she offered.

The glasses rose and chimed again. Via nodded in her shy, inebriated way. Jane sank to her seat.

"Speech!" Sean called.

"Yeah, speech! Speech!"

It took some doing, but eventually Via relented. Her old Nehru jacket shone in the low light.

"Thank you all for coming," she said. "It means a lot to me to have you here."

They nodded, pleased with themselves for being dutiful.

"I went through the attic recently, and I packed up a box for each of you, of all your old things. They're out in the hall, and I want you to take them home. I split up the photo albums so you'll each have pictures."

She sat down. That was that. It was hard to drink to, but they did. *How very Via*, Jane thought. Welcoming them and turning them out in the same breath. She hadn't loved Jane as much as Jane loved Emily, not by a long shot.

"Photos!" Caroline said, rubbing her hands. "What do you think, kids?"

"Presents—"

"Cake—"

Perhaps Via had become a better mother after Jane. No one else seemed to be waiting for the ax to fall.

"To Via!" Greer said.

"To Via!"

Jane heard Emily's voice, singled it out from all the others. It wasn't difficult, considering it was the loudest one.

THE OLDER TEENS escaped to a movie, so it was only the younger cousins who lay together in the circle of sleeping bags, looking up at the sky for shooting stars. Emily was still wild, and rolled into a giggling ball when Jane bent down to kiss her good night.

"Call if you need me," Jane said, ostensibly to all of them. There was a vast depletion of energy in the circle; she'd pulled the children out of their private world. "Have fun," she added sheepishly. One of them said *good night, Aunt Jane*. Otherwise there was silence as they waited for her to leave.

Jane walked across the dew-wet grass up to the house, which loomed like a cruise ship anchored in a dark bay. She found the group in the living room, having after-after-dinner drinks. Everyone had scavenged the photographs from their boxes and were using them as prompts for reminiscences and loud, exuberantly told stories. Jane had taken her box down to her tent, thinking she could look through it if she woke up early. It didn't matter; there were enough pictures without hers.

To Jane's surprise, Via was present. Normally, she and Ned went to bed shortly after dinner. Sean must have persuaded her to stay up.

Francis had changed into his silk robe and embroidered slippers. Everyone else was still dressed.

Eventually, the show-and-tell was over, and they leaned back into the comfortable sofas. "I'm going to go up," Karen, Alex's wife, said. "See you all tomorrow."

They smiled at her and poured another round. Jane declined; the wine she'd drunk during dinner had been plenty, and spoiling in its quality. As Sean walked the bottle around, he also turned off most of the lamps. The siblings weren't in a hurry to separate; who knew when they'd ever be together again?

Sean was chewing gum, which meant he was trying to quit smoking again. Jane smelled the scent of Juicy Fruit as he leaned over her, and her mouth watered. Juicy Fruit! Emlin teaching her to ride a bike. Grand holding her raft steady, waiting for the right wave on which to send her sailing into shore. Nonny asking for help with a necklace clasp.

"Get away from me with that gum." She batted at him. She ached.

"I'm stuffed," Alex said. "You sure ordered well, Mom."

"It's one of my old-age talents," Via said. She liked to flirt with her sons.

They could hear the children laughing. Paul volunteered to go help them settle down.

"How about some music?" Sean said.

"Sure. Put on what you gave me," Via said.

Sean's present to her had been a boxed set of Beatles CDs. "Okay." He left for the den.

Caroline's pink sandals dangled from her bare feet. "This is nice," she said.

It was a generic remark. They barely knew each other in any present sense.

"It is," Francis agreed.

Jane looked at him for signs of drollery, but he was merely sleepy. Sometimes she forgot he was nearing seventy, and that, sharp as he was, his body sought comfort and rest.

The music came on. It was the Beatles' early music. "She Loves You," raucous and bright.

"Turn it down," Via hissed loudly.

The volume sank.

"My guys love the Beatles," Alex said.

Jane wished she had a dollar for every time she'd heard that remark over the last few years. Among the parents at Emily's school, it was a point of pride for the children to like the Beatles.

"Poor George Harrison," Caroline said. "It's a good example, though, for kids not to smoke."

Jane and Francis exchanged glances. Poor Caroline's kids.

Sean walked in and stood with his hands on his hips. "Remember the night we watched the Beatles on Ed Sullivan?"

Jane stared. No one had ever mentioned it again.

"The night your Dad died." Mary Beth leaned forward, elbows on knees. Aside from being inhumanly competent, she also liked to call a spade a spade. "If you guys don't mind, I'd like to hear about it. I'm not really clear on what happened."

Silence. Jane didn't have to look at Francis this time. The request would bother him on two counts; his sense of propriety, and his preference for entertaining talk.

Jane was torn. She wanted to be in league with him, but she was also curious. No one else she knew remembered her father.

"There's not much to tell," Alex said. "He had a car accident."

"Yes, but . . ." Jane heard herself say. They all looked at her.

"But what?"

"Things happened that night."

"I don't remember anything," Caroline said.

"You were only four," Jane said. "Do you remember seeing the Beatles?"

She shook her head. "All I remember is the next day when Mom told us. She called us all into Nonny's kitchen. I was confused because we'd just had lunch a little while earlier. She told us all to sit down and then said our father was dead."

"That must have been awful," Mary Beth said.

"Sean ran out in the snow," Jane told her. "No boots, no coat, nothing."

Mary Beth took Sean's hand.

It was now or no other time. Jane had gone over it on her

own and in therapy, but it had always been a taboo in the family. It was the night by which they were bound to each other, and the agreement had been to forget, or at least to not mention it. She could see from the faces that no one had forgotten. They were haunted, too. Not as thoroughly as she'd been. They'd all managed to marry and raise the size and shape of families they wanted. But there was a difference between them. Their consciences were clear.

"Does anyone remember what happened with the telephone?" Jane asked.

"The telephone?" Alex's foot began to jiggle. He didn't like to talk about anything serious, not with the family.

Francis glanced at Jane and leaned forward. He understood her need. "The phone got knocked off the hook, didn't it?"

"Knocked off, or someone took it off," Jane said.

"Why would anyone do that?" Caroline asked. She looked around for agreement that it was a ridiculous notion.

"Because we didn't want him to go back to the hospital," Jane said. She glanced at Via. Via rocked gently, her gaze lowered.

Caroline raised her open palms, as if this proved her point. "Of course he was going to go back to the hospital! He was a doctor!"

"Wait a minute," Sean said. "I remember that. We wanted him to watch the Ed Sullivan show with us."

"The idea was a joke, but then the phone did turn up off the hook." Francis directed his comment to Mary Beth.

"Well," Via said. She pushed her hands against her thighs and stood up. "I don't remember any of it."

"I know what you mean. I'm lucky if I can remember my name at my age," Francis said, attempting to lighten the conversation. He could tell Via had had enough.

Jane wasn't as fluid. She wanted to follow through. She realized she'd been waiting for this moment for years. "You told him I took it off the hook," she said to Via.

Via stood still, her cheeks drooping. "Well."

"Why did you say that?" Jane asked.

"Leave her alone," Alex said. "It's her birthday."

"Yeah, Jane, let it go," Caroline said. "You always think you're better than everyone else."

Jane was shocked. The accusation was so monumentally off the mark that she didn't know how to respond. Alex glanced at Via, then, and Jane understood. They'd talked about her when she was out of the room. What had she done? Something they'd interpreted as offensive. She considered asking, but she knew it didn't really matter what it was. No matter what she said, or did, that night was such a part of her that she embodied it. She was the conscience of the past, its reminder. She looked like Emlin—and now she was almost the age he'd been when he died. She must resemble him more than ever. She was an accusation without her ever saying a word.

"I didn't bring it up," she said.

It didn't matter. She personified it. No one would look at her.

The despair she felt at the moment made her realize that in spite of the nervousness she'd felt that morning, she'd still had hope. In spite of everything, she was still the girl who wanted the happy family.

"Who took the phone off the hook?" she asked. The only hope left was to set the record straight.

Via stood up. "I'm going to bed."

"Oh, come on, Mom," Caroline said. "Stay."

She waved her hand. Her head was bobbing. "No, no, it's way past my bedtime."

"Great," Alex said to Jane. "You know, you're really—"

"Come on, now," Francis said. "It's a legitimate question. Maybe it would be—"

"No!" someone screamed.

Jane froze. The scream had come not from among those gathered, but from outside. Everyone began to rise, but she remained still, alert, her adrenaline pumping. If she wasn't sure what was going on, her body knew.

"No!" The second scream was easier to identify. It was Emily.

. . .

Paul knelt above her. He raised his palms in a gesture of helplessness. "She was asleep. I don't know, she must have had a nightmare."

"It's all right," Jane said.

Emily was sitting up. Her hair hung like a curtain past her cheeks. Jane knew she was embarrassed.

"Is everything okay?" Caroline asked. Jane had run so fast that it took the others a few seconds to catch up. "Is anyone hurt?"

"Nope. Everything's fine," Jane said. She picked up Emily, who wrapped her legs around Jane's waist. She still had her face hidden. The family went off to bed, relieved it was only a bad dream.

Jane carried her daughter across the meadow. The moon had risen and hung low in the sky. It was big enough that its face showed. The quiet night was alive; beyond her own swishing footsteps, Jane could hear throaty calls and the scratch of nails on tree bark. Her espadrilles dampened.

"Aren't I heavy?" Emily asked.

"Not for me. Go back to sleep."

"I'm not tired."

They crawled inside and Jane turned on the flashlight lantern.

"What did you dream about, anyway?" She began to undress.

Emily looked around. "Hey, what's this?" She pointed to the box. She doesn't want to tell me, Jane thought.

"Old things of mine that Via had in her attic. She's been cleaning it out." Jane buttoned her pajamas and put on a zip-up sweatshirt. She felt cold when she was tired.

Emily opened the box. "Let's see what we've got here." In spite of the dream, the freewheeling evening with her cousins had emboldened her.

The photographs were on the top: Emily pulled them out

and set them aside. The rest was papers and letters, all crammed together in no order. A political science paper. An invitation to the one and only coming-out party of Jane's very antiestablishment coming-out year. College notebooks. Ticket stubs from rock concerts, programs from plays. Letters she'd received during the year she lived in London. And a packet of letters wrapped with a thin ribbon. Letters she'd completely forgotten. Letters from Clay. Jane put those on her sleeping bag.

"What's this?" Emily asked.

She held up a notebook. On the cover was a faded piece of construction paper with a drawing and a title. "Poems and Thoughts."

"Those are things I wrote when I was little."

Emily opened it. "How little?"

"Nine."

Emily looked up at her.

"Not so little, is it?" said Jane.

"Not really." Emily turned the pages, looking briefly at the pictures, getting an overview as they'd taught her do to at school. She stopped near the end. "What's this about?"

Jane crawled to where she could see it. Instantly, she remembered doing the pencil drawing of a newborn; she'd been at Susan Roberts's house, on a snowy afternoon. *That* afternoon. She and Emily read the poem at the same time. "I used to think I remembered being born," Jane explained.

"You did?"

"Uh-huh. I couldn't believe no one else seemed to."

"I do."

"Thank you," Jane said, embracing Emily's thin shoulders. "You don't have to say you believe me, though."

"No—I mean I remember being born, too." Emily pulled her nightgown tight over her bent knees. "I dream about it. About him," she said.

"Him?" Jane automatically thought she meant Emlin. That was who Jane dreamed about.

"You know. Him. My brother." She was quiet for a moment. She leaned her head against her bent legs. "Sometimes I talk to him."

Jane got gooseflesh and felt the hard, tight beat of her shocked heart.

"What do you say?"

"I don't know. I tell him I'm sorry."

"Sorry?"

"That he died."

The phrase thumped. He died. Jane had grown around the words, like a vine around fence slats. And so had Emily.

"Is that what your nightmare was about?" she asked quietly.

Emily nodded. "I have it a lot."

"Why haven't you told me?"

She lowered her gaze and shrugged.

"Em, you can tell me anything. You know that, don't you?"

Emily's shadow bobbed against the wall of the tent.

"So what is it? Please, Em."

Jane wanted to see her child's face; she reached out and pushed the curtain of hair aside, then followed, with a light touch, the line from Emily's temple down her cheek to her chin, which she lifted gently. Emily was rocking herself and rubbing her feet together like a cricket. She glanced at Jane several times before finally succumbing to a complete gaze. Jane didn't take her hand away, and Emily wrapped her fingers in a loose bracelet around Jane's wrist.

"You try so hard, Mom. It makes me sad."

As her eyes filled, Jane automatically dropped her head to hide her distress. She'd never wanted Emily to see her despair and had worked hard to protect her from it. She'd thought she was doing the right thing; but it hadn't protected her, had it? Instead, it had taught Emily to hide her own sorrow. To hide the truth. Perhaps it was time to do things differently. Jane turned back to Emily and allowed her face to grow wet without rubbing it away.

"Do you feel guilty about it?" she asked. "About him, I mean?"

Silence.

"It had nothing to do with you. I promise."

Emily wasn't convinced. Jane could feel her skepticism.

"How could it have anything to do with you? You weren't even born." It was laughable. Though not at all funny.

"I don't know. I just feel like it did."

Jane knew that feeling. A sense of responsibility that spread beyond its natural boundaries. A kudzu of the spirit. "I always believed it was my fault that my father died."

"I thought he had a car accident."

"He did. I still blamed myself."

"What did Via say to you?"

"We never talked about it," Jane said.

Emily nodded. This made sense to her. "She tries, too."

Jane considered this. Could it be true? How did she try? She remembered how Via used to make chicken with sour cream and coffee mousse for Emlin, and how she'd taught Jane to knit and make beds, read and do flower arrangements. How she jumped up to answer the phone and laughed at her friends' jokes. How she gave each of the children a section of the garden to grow what they wished.

"You're right," she said. The fact was that Jane was too much like Emlin to understand Via's efforts. Via wasn't a serious person. But she did try.

"I think I've made a mistake, though. From now on I want to tell you how I feel about things."

"Okay, Mommy."

"Okay, then."

Jane lay down and beckoned Emily to lie beside her. They wrapped their arms around each other and she smelled Emily's stiff, sweaty hair. There was no time like the present to live up to her vow. "I miss your brother, too," she said. "I was going to name him Emlin. Then Colette would have been your first name instead of your middle name."

Emily yawned. "I don't think I seem like a Colette."

"No. I don't think so either."

She ran her hand over Emily's fuzzy hairline, the same gesture over and over.

"I call him Leo," Emily said.

Jane knew why. Leonardo DiCaprio. He was Emily's George Harrison.

"I like that," Jane said.

"It's odd, Mom. He doesn't mind being dead. I'm the one who minds."

Jane couldn't speak.

"Do you mind if I stay here a few days?" Emily asked. "Elizabeth is staying, and Greer wants to."

"What about camp?"

"Did you sign me up for this week yet?"

"No."

"I'd rather stay with Via and Ned. It's really fun here. We're going to chip the garnets out of the rocks in the stream and sell them."

"Are you sure you're ready for it?"

"It's not like staying with a friend. These are my relatives."

"I'll think about it," Jane said.

"Mom?"

"Yes?"

"Do you think my father ever wonders about me?"

"Do you wonder about him?"

"Sometimes."

Like tonight. After a day of seeing her cousins with their fathers.

"I bet he does," Jane said.

"That's good."

Emily rolled into her sleep position. On her side, with her knees pulled up, just like Jane.

. . .

When Emily was asleep, Jane opened a packet of letters she'd spotted at the bottom of the box. They were musty and

247

growing brittle, but their words were still fresh—Clay had a powerful style, she had to give him that. The letters had all been written to convince her to change her mind about leaving him. From London he made rational arguments. After he moved back to California, he began to write more about himself, funny descriptions of his days, his friends, the city— sentences that made her press her hand to her mouth to keep from laughing aloud. She knew she'd read them, but she didn't remember their contents. She'd worked hard not to pay attention.

In his second-to-last letter, he wrote that he loved her, and that he'd been an asshole not to say so before. If she wanted a commitment—hey, what kind of Californian would he be if he wasn't willing to believe in a reinterpretation of old material? As for children . . .

Persuade me. Argue with me. Refuse to take no for an answer. That's where you went wrong; you believed in me so much that you believed the crap I said, too. But think about it—if I could be persuaded to get married in order to buy a car, don't you think I could be convinced to make a few plans with *you?*

She thought of those months, of all the energy she put into expunging him from her being, until she didn't even talk about him to herself. He was taboo.

What have I done? she thought.

She wrapped the letters up again and laid them carefully at the bottom of the box. Her fingers touched another envelope she hadn't seen before. She shone the flashlight on it. It was addressed to her at 34 Willow Lane. The envelope flap was lacy, old ladyish; Grandmother M., she wondered? She pulled out the card. Roses and hearts and a cherub and a flowery script declaring a Happy Valentine's Day. The message, written in a crabbed doctor's handwriting, with a blotchy pen, read:

For Jane, From your loving Daddy.

SLEEPING IN?" Caroline asked. "I can't remember the last time I got up past seven."

Jane forced herself to smile. "You're an example to us all."

Caroline nodded. She wore golf clothes. A skort. Jane was sure Francis had lamented it already.

"We've been reading your book," Mary Beth said.

Jane walked up the stone steps to the terrace. She guessed from the position of the sun it was almost ten. She'd woken up to the scent of grass and warm light just on the other side of her eyelids. She was alone in the tent, and for a moment she reverted to her habit of panic: Emily, danger, death?

Possible, but not likely. She had to remind herself of that.

In fact, Emily was sitting on a chaise, playing cards with Via, looking fed and content. In no danger at all. "My book?"

Mary Beth held up the "The Happy MacMillans."

"Where did you get that? I completely forgot about it."

"It was in my box," Sean said. "Via didn't know whose it was. But I remembered when you wrote it. You used to work on it by flashlight under the covers."

Via didn't know who wrote it?

"It's really good, Mom," Emily said. "We think you should publish it."

"I have connections," Francis said. He winked at Jane and sipped his Bloody Mary.

"The only thing is," Mary Beth said, "we can't figure out why you called it "The Happy MacMillans" when these people are constantly in a hurricane or being surrounded by wolf packs or burglarized."

These people.

"It was meant to be a study of how a family pulls together to handle adversity. It's a fantasy. Pure fiction. I made it up. We all know real families don't behave that way."

Francis gave her a warning look. What did it matter what she said, though? They'd made up their minds about her long ago.

"Oh, I don't know." Mary Beth put the book down and pushed it a few inches away from her. Jane thought she probably didn't want to risk starting things again.

"It reminded me of the Brady Bunch," Alex said. "Maybe you should work for Disney, or something." He had his bare feet up on the iron-mesh coffee table. The hair on his ankles had been rubbed away by decades of lisle socks.

"Great idea. Although I think my worldview may have altered a tad since I wrote that." Jane walked over to the big table and poured a cup of coffee. It appeared she was the last one up. The table was strewn with used plates; in the trees above the terrace, birds, mainly crows, eyed the leftover croissant crumbs. She gathered them onto one plate and placed it on the wall at a safe distance from the humans.

"Did you sleep well?" Via asked. She never remembered in the morning what had gone on the night before. Every day was a do-over; every night history repeated itself.

"Very well, thanks," she said.

Emily beamed. She gets anxious when everyone isn't nice to each other, Jane thought. Perhaps it was genetic, a trait inherited from Nonny.

"There was a review today that might interest you," Francis said.

Jane took a seat near the coffee table where the newspaper was scattered.

"Oh?"

Mary Beth grew animated again. She scrambled for the book review and held it up. *Letters of Explanation* was on the cover. "It got a great review," she said.

Never read reviews, Clay had advised her. But that was advice to a writer, and she hadn't become one, at least not the kind who might be inhibited by a review. Politely, she reached for the magazine. It would be more noteworthy if she wasn't curious.

She was curious.

She began to read the review and was smiling at a line that referred to Clay's orneriness—hadn't she used that the word for him herself?—when Sean lowered the section he was reading and faced her.

"Jane—guess what? Mary Beth and I were talking last night, and I remembered something. I think I was the one who took the phone off the hook."

He spoke casually, but it was clear he was tense. Did he

really think Jane would be angry at him? She felt a wave of sorrow pass through her for how much in her family was misunderstood.

"Thank you," she said. She gave him as much of a smile as she could muster.

He laced his fingers over his abdomen, as if to protect his guts. "I didn't mean any harm."

"No. You were a child." She glanced over at Via. "Did you hear that, Mother?"

Via was sitting as if in a saddle, her thin legs straddling the chaise. She stared down at her cards. "Mmnn." She picked up a card and moved it over to Emily's side. "A ten on your nine."

Emily tapped her fingers against her lips and stared at her cards. Jane tried to read more of the review, but her heart was thick and so loud she couldn't concentrate. She closed the pages and set them on the table.

"Was it Sean?" she asked.

No response. She visored a hand over her eyes, but Via's head was bent so low Jane couldn't see her expression.

"Mother?"

Via snapped a card from her hand, then another. "Yes?"

Jane tried to stay calm, but her leg began to swing. "I asked if it was Sean."

"What about him?"

"He thinks he took the phone off the hook. You told Emlin that I did it. I'd like to know the truth."

Via laid her cards down. "I really don't remember anything about it."

Emily laid down a card in a gesture of triumph. "I win!"

Via nodded. "You're getting good enough to really play with." She didn't look Jane's way.

"What shall we play now?" Emily asked.

"That's enough for me," Via said.

Mary Beth beckoned to Emily. "Let's go find Greer, shall we?"

Emily looked at Jane for approval. Jane nodded. They went into the house.

Via stood and stretched. "I'm going for a walk."

"Wait," Jane said. "I want you to try. To remember."

They all looked at her. She held the edge of the chair with all her strength. Not a poker face. Not rising above it.

"Drop it, Jane," Sean said. "It was a long time ago."

Jane was furious. Drop it?

Via shook her head in annoyance, as if the subject had been discussed ad infinitum. She walked briskly away. For a moment, out of her old habit of witnessing, Jane watched her go. Then she jumped up.

. . .

She caught up with Via in the driveway.

"I'm coming with you."

Via tipped her head to the side, accepting but not condoning. Jane felt less angry after the brief run, and slightly embarrassed by the intensity of her need to know the truth. Intensity wasn't something she normally displayed to Via; or anyone, for that matter. A visit with the family brought it out.

For a few moments they walked in silence. They headed out to the road. The lawns beside the drive had already begun to gather dead leaves.

"So Emily had a nightmare last night? I didn't want to ask her about it."

"She did. Apparently, she's been having a lot of them."

"Has she? Why?"

Jane wanted to say, *never mind, it's nothing, back-to-school nerves*. She didn't trust Via to be a good listener. Whenever she'd tried to discuss a concern about Emily, Via veered toward quick explanations; a flaw in her diet; those other, unknown genes. But Emily was a common ground. A place to begin.

"She dreams about her brother."

"Her brother?"

"The child I lost. She dreams about him the way I used to dream about my father."

Via disappeared. It took Jane a second to realize she'd dropped to her haunches. When she straightened, she was holding the plastic bottle holders from a six-pack. "These are deadly to water birds," Via said. "They get tangled in them and drown. The thing to do is to cut them up in little pieces and put them out with the recycling." She folded the plastic and tucked it in her pocket.

Jane gaped at her. It wasn't going to be possible to hide her feelings. "Did you know I used to be haunted by my father?"

Via motioned for them to keep walking. They turned

left at the end of her property, down the country road. "Haunted?" she said as she twisted around to look for the source of a bird call.

"He'd appear to me. Mostly in my dreams. For a while, he hovered at my ceiling at night and told me what I'd done wrong that day. Then sometimes he'd pop up when I was out in the world. He was a ghost."

"Well, I don't know anything about that," Via said. She reached out to deadhead a rhododendron.

"You never dreamed about him?"

"Jane, don't."

"Don't what?"

Via threw up her hands. "I know it was hard. Don't you think I know? I lost him, too. But you never think about that. You've always blamed me."

"Blamed *you?*"

"He was my husband," Via said. Her voice broke.

Jane instantly yearned to console her. Her mother's sorrow was unbearable. "We all lost him," Jane said. "Him and more than him. We lost the family."

Via wiped at her eyes. She sniffed. "That's a funny thing to say, when we're all together."

Jane felt rebuffed and looked away. On the other side of the street stood a huge new house. Bunches of marigolds had been perfunctorily planted in dull clumps along the walk. Their literalness maddened her.

"We can't talk about what we went through. That's not what I'd call a family."

"Everyone else gets along."

"They're being polite. They haven't seen each other as a group in years."

Via shook her head. "That's not my fault."

Jane trembled. What chance was there for understanding if Via denied Jane's perceptions? This is what happened between her and her parents, Jane thought. This is the crippling haunting—the ghost of harm done, coming back and back and back. Via didn't know she'd taken on Nonny and Grand's worst aspect. The willful absenting of the soul at crucial moments, so that life consisted only of what was comfortable. On the eve of their daughters' weddings, Victorian mothers put it like this: Just close your eyes and think of England. Jane wasn't sure what Via wanted her to think of, but Via clearly believed Jane should close her eyes.

"I'm talking about the waste," Jane said. "We could know each other." She thought of her talk in the tent with Emily. How privileged she'd felt.

"We do," Via said. "We do. But you want more than that."

"That's true," Jane said.

Via looked at her in surprise. She'd expected an argument. Jane's admission disarmed her. She didn't understand it was another form of argument. "I know it hurt you, Jane. You were close to him. Too close, I always believed. I never saw a man so interested in a baby. It was as if I didn't exist after you were born." She laughed, although they were both acutely aware that it wasn't amusing.

"You were jealous," Jane said.

"You would be, too," Via said hotly, defensively. "You don't know what it's like."

"No."

"You have complete control of Emily. You don't have to do what anyone else says. You don't have to cope with losing a husband and having miserable kids to deal with. You don't have to answer to anyone."

She's still jealous, Jane thought. *She believes I have freedom.*

Via pointed left. They turned onto a dirt path that led between the properties and down to the stream, back in the direction of the house.

"Why did you say I took the phone off the hook?"

"Dammit, Jane—I don't remember what happened that night. But if I told him it was you, I'd guess it was because I thought that wouldn't make him mad."

The light came through the trees in discreet gems.

"Sometimes I actually believed I did it," Jane said. "I never blamed you for his death. I blamed myself."

"Well, I'm sorry about that." Via shook her head. "All this time I thought you were angry at me."

Survivor's guilt, Jane thought. Via had used Jane as a mirror to see it in herself. Jane had seen a ghost. Emily had apologized over and over for a death that was never her fault.

They came parallel to the back of the house. The group on the terrace were in view.

"Maybe we should have talked more," Via said. "But it's too late now."

Jane looked over at her family. Yes, she thought.

And no.

JANE LAY AWAKE. It was no use. She sat up and turned on the lamp.

It was Wednesday night, three days after she'd left Via's, and she'd been agitated ever since. Partly because she'd never been separated from Emily for this long, and the absence left her bereft. Partly because of the sorrow she felt about her family, and her final loss of hope that they'd ever be truly close. Partly, too, because she'd been trying to write a letter, but she couldn't figure out what to say.

She swung her legs over the edge of the bed and felt for her espadrilles. She wore a tee shirt and underwear, but in spite of the shades being up, she made no attempt to cover herself further; if there was a voyeur out there who wanted to see a forty-five-year-old woman's legs, so be it. The dining room table had become a temporary desk. She'd taken out her good fountain pen and her good paper, many sheets of which were crumpled in the scrap basket. It had crossed her mind that it would be practical, both to conserve the good paper and to employ orderly work habits, to write a rough draft on loose-leaf paper, but there was nothing about this letter that was practical. No, that wasn't true; it was an explanation, which was a practical entity; but the content was wild. Uncaptured, as yet.

She reread her latest beginning and groaned. Too stiff. She measured coffee, enough for a pot. She made it for the scent as much as anything, to disguise the summer tang of urine that rose from the hot pavement.

Before she sat down, she stuck her head into Emily's room as she'd done a hundred times since Sunday. It was all she could do outside of calling, which she did once a day, in the evening. It would surely alarm Emily if she called as much as she wanted to. It was a discipline not to call; she'd always sought out her disciplines. How many plans had she made and lists had she written in her life? Little, considered plans, like doing her laundry every Thursday afternoon; and big, unconscious ones, such as having a child without a father, so that what happened to her couldn't happen again, not while she had anything to say about it. Good plans and not-so-good plans, all in an attempt to erect a bulwark against sorrow— which wasn't possible anyway. Families shattered. Friendships failed. Love foundered on fear and misunderstanding.

She poured her coffee and sat down. Marmalade rubbed against her leg and then jumped up on the table and settled on his side to watch. "Don't expect much," she told him. The fresh sheet of stationery looked huge and blank. *Dear Clay*, she wrote, and immediately frowned—already she hated it. The word "dear" sounded cloying. She tore up the page. All the lines she'd thought of after she read his book escaped her. She was out of practice in writing her thoughts down. As for poetry—the last time she'd written any was the day Em was born; in Jane's drugged state after the cesarean section, she'd scribbled a few poems that made about as much sense as drugged poems usually do, and that was that. If she had any regrets about not becoming a poet, they were so far down her list that they didn't bother her. She was pleased, though, to have "The Happy MacMillans" back. Mary Beth had been right that the family was unusually beset by peril. Had she sensed a disaster coming? She couldn't remember. Certainly, she'd sensed a threat. The more interesting question had to do with why she'd imagined there was such a thing as a happy family. Where had she gotten that idea? Actually, it wasn't much of a mystery; there were fairy tales, handsome princes, and happily ever after; but there were also the moments when the dream came true. Sometimes, in the morning, when Via made pancakes and Emlin sat reading the paper, while the children made faces at each other across the table. Or when they were down at the shore, and everyone was on the beach, including Nonny and Grand, and the children were given permission to buy a Coke after a morning of jumping the waves; when the Beatles made their first appearance on Ed Sullivan and they all watched together. They'd been happy then. Her mistake had been to expect such moments could last.

The idea of a happy family came from the same place as her idea about finding a soul mate. The place where she'd first lived, in complete communion with Via. Nothing had come between them then. When she was born, and the connection was broken, she began to pine.

She remembered it. She and Via had been happy. She and Clay had had their moments of happiness, too.

She poured another cup of coffee. Perhaps the easiest way to go about writing would be to describe what her life was like. Let him judge whether or not she was better off without him. He would, anyway, no doubt.

She was walking back to the dining room when she stopped abruptly. Someone else was in the apartment. The presence was palpable. She tried to stand utterly still, so as not to be detected, but inside herself she heard her blood rush, and the metallic tingling of her nerves. A minute passed. She took a step. Nothing. She began to doubt her perception; there'd been no noise, after all, she'd just had a feeling. She took another step.

"Hello?"

She felt silly once she'd said it. Was an intruder really going to answer her? There was no intruder, or anything else. She was alone. She walked back to the table and sat down again.

She wanted to apologize to Clay, to say she'd been young, and impatient, and full of ideas about how things should be that differed from his own. She was sure he knew that, but it bore writing down. She picked up the pen, and starting a third of the way down the page (she'd put a salutation in later), she began to write.

I'm sorry I didn't try harder to understand . . .

She froze. There it was again. The presence.

"Hello?"

Slowly, cautiously, she got up and went to the telephone. As quietly as she could, she lifted it off the hook. To her relief, there was a dial tone. No one had cut the wires. If she needed to, she could call for help.

It's nothing, she told herself. A phantom of insomnia. Yet it had thrown her off her task. She thought perhaps she'd lie down for a while, and then try again.

She planned to get in her own bed but, automatically, she stopped at the door of Emily's room. From the doorway Jane could smell Emily's scent in the small space. Her skin; old people and children both gave off strong odors from their skin. Jane walked in and, without turning on the lights, lay on the bed. It was an odd feeling; she never lay here. When Emily was lonely, she came to Jane's bigger bed; this one was too small for two people. Jane tried to locate a trench in the mattress in the shape of Emily's body, but Emily was too slight to have changed its contours. But the pillow smelled of her hair, a mixture of tropical flowers. She pulled her braid forward over her shoulder and settled on her back with the phone at her side, just in case.

She looked at the shadows. When Em was younger, she'd often been afraid of them, but she hadn't mentioned it in a while. She was learning how to cope.

Jane shifted her gaze to the ceiling. Emlin used to appear at the ceiling of her childhood room. He hovered like a sky diver with his arms and legs out, his tie hanging straight down. She'd been so afraid of him. He knew too much about her, everything. He knew that in spite of her best efforts, she hadn't been able to help him.

"I'm sorry," she said.

She heard her own voice speak aloud; and then, not with her ears but in another manner of hearing, there came a response.

It's all right.

A FEW WEEKS LATER, at his house in Los Angeles, Clay West received a letter that had been forwarded by his publisher.

Dear Clay,

I read your book and thought about whether or not I've been better off without you. I decided the question was, as you would say, wrong-headed. Just because you don't see somebody doesn't mean they aren't in your life.

Your old friend, Jane MacLeod

The furrow in his brow deepened as he thought about it. Then he nodded. He had to admit, she made a good point.

Think of England
Synopsis

From an acknowledged master of short fiction comes a deeply affecting novel about a thoughtful girl's journey into adulthood. When the narrative opens in 1964, Jane MacLeod is a precocious nine-year-old, troubled by her parents' misery and trying to will her family into happiness. But soon her hopes are dashed by a tragedy that is to haunt her for many years to come. Jane is twenty-three when she travels to London to forge a new path for herself. After befriending Nigel and Colette, whose creativity and unfettered lifestyle inspire her, she meets a tall writer named Clay, who reawakens her longing for a happy life—but again she is disillusioned. Decades pass before Jane, now a single mother with a daughter of her own, is able to come to terms with her past.

Discussion points

1. "Set me as a seal upon your heart . . . for love is as strong as death, passion as fierce as the grave." These words from the Song of Solomon serve as an epigraph to *Think of England*. Why do you think the author chose this quotation? What role do love and passion play in the story? What kinds of love prove most powerful?

2. Split into three sections that take place many years apart, the novel has an unusual and intriguing structure.

Why do you suppose Dark chose to tell her story this way? How do the leaps in time enrich our understanding of the characters and themes?

3. The young Jane shows signs of a maturity far beyond her years. "Oh, Jane," her father says. "You know too much." But in London in her twenties, she often feels naïve and insecure, especially in the face of Colette's blithe sophistication. Discuss the tension between innocence and knowingness in the book, both between characters and within Jane herself.

4. Via "championed the idea of work and women getting out of the house, but in truth she'd have been more gratified by having her husband in the nest, with nobody going anywhere." How do Via's ambivalent feelings about family life influence Jane's choices?

5. England "was a country obsessed with merging the past with the present. The opposite of me, Jane thought." What does Jane mean by this?

6. Deeply disappointed by the way the life of the MacLeods has turned out, Jane comes to think of her friends in London as her surrogate family. Years later, she starts a new family of a very atypical kind. Discuss her changing perceptions of the concept of family.

7. Jane comes from an upper-middle-class background, and she seems to feel conflicted about her relatively privi-

leged place in society. Nigel and Colette also have tangled relationships with money. How do attitudes about class influence the behavior of the characters in *Think of England*?

8. While in London, Jane witnesses a slashing at a punk rock concert and a bombing in the street. What makes these violent scenes so effective? How do Jane's reactions shed light on her character?

9. Why do you think Jane is drawn to Clay West? Do his theories on writing help or hurt her work? How does their relationship ultimately resolve itself?

10. What is Colette's role in the novel? Did your opinion of her change over the course of the narrative? What do you think happened to her?

11. Why do you think Jane decides to leave London? How has she changed since arriving there? What about her has stayed the same?

12. In the last section of the book, Jane confronts her family with a question that has been weighing on her for over three decades: "Who took the phone off the hook?" Who do you think did?